I0555929

THE CORE
Equilibrium Series, Book I
Kate Thomas

The Core, Equilibrium I

Copyright © 2015 by Kate Thomas

All rights reserved. This book or any portion thereof may not be reproduced or used in any manner whatsoever without the express written permission of the publisher except for the use of brief quotations in a book review.

The novel is a work of fiction. Names, characters, places and plot are all either products of the author's imagination or used fictitiously. Any resemblance to actual events, locales, or persons – living or dead – is purely coincidental.

First Edition.

ISBN –978-1927940297

Editor: Nicole Hewitt
Cover Designer: Kellie Dennis,
Book Covers by Design

To my mom, who devours my books and gets ticked when they're over.

Love you more than words could express.
I thank God for you all the time.

Chapter **One**

"You do realize that there is absolutely no chance of us actually getting away with this, right?" Ellie whispered loudly in the small confines of the car.

"There's no need to whisper. We're in a car by ourselves, Elle." Jacob kept his eyes on the car in front of them, the large figure of his sister's boss moving languidly from the Lincoln to cross the busy street. "Besides, it's the holidays, and it's far too busy in this neighborhood for Mr. Kelley to notice us."

A soft sigh resounded beside him, and sounds of fidgeting filled the air. Ellie was rarely the type to be nervous or overcome with emotion of any sort. If anyone was capable of a stakeout operation, it was most certainly his twin sister. She was only a few minutes older than him, but years ahead in maturity and intellectual curiosities, to be sure. He smiled as he felt the overwhelming heat of her stare. Paying her no attention would be more fun than giving in to her well-founded fits of worry.

"I know you know I'm looking at you, Jacob." Her punch was much too light to be anything but playful.

He glanced her way only briefly, a smirk on his mouth his only response. He was used to responding non-verbally.

"It's not me you should be watching, but your illustrious boss. I didn't come out in the freezing cold to spend my night in a car, hanging out with my bratty older sister. I came to see if I could help you get a few answers. Pay attention!" He turned the heater up, and the previously fogged window cleared, showing a row of beautifully decorated mansions.

Christmas was in full effect on Ebert Street, and the wealthy citizens of the neighborhood spent loads outdoing their friends and family. Their study for the evening was a Mr. David Kelley, Ellie's boss for the last two years. He was an investor of other people's money, a financial advisor by some standards and a bookie by others.

"I am paying attention, but I don't know what you expect to find by sitting outside of a luxurious home in the middle of winter. It's the holidays, so yes, David goes to parties and wines and dines the rich and famous. What did you think we would find tonight?" She added softly, "I didn't even ask you to come."

Jacob turned to face his sister. "You most certainly did ask me to come. You've been bitching for the last two years about your boss's oddities, and it was you that wanted to start looking into his personal life."

"Not his personal life, but I wanted to see what it is that he does with his time." She turned to face him as well, a defiant look spreading across her features. "How does someone make more money than God and never really DO anything? Besides, you've been wanting a reason to see the Christmas lights in Westchester for years."

"Christmas lights, pff …" He rolled his eyes. "I want to hear it or I'm leaving."

"Hear what?" Confusion spread across her features.

"I want to hear that you asked me to come, and that this is your operation."

"Don't be ridiculous, Jacob."

He turned to face the windshield and moved to put the car in reverse before her hand clamped down on his shoulder. "Fine. Fine. You're such a child, but if I need to say it, I will. I wanted you to help me figure out who my boss really is and what he's up to. There, I said it."

Jacob put his hands in his lap and looked back at his sister. "Why?"

"Why what?"

He sighed before continuing. "Why did you want me to help you? You've been with Mr. Kelley for the last two years. Why now?"

Ellie began fidgeting again, her eyes moving from his face to focus somewhere in her lap as her fingers brushed by one another. She didn't speak for a minute, and he didn't give her comfort or afford her any alternative besides answering him. He'd been pulled into this unfounded operation, and he deserved a reason for the sudden change in her behavior. She glanced at him and then exhaled loudly, as if realizing that she was, in fact, going to have to share some information that she must've wanted to keep to herself.

"Fine. I wanted to know what he was doing because he's so mysterious, and I've yet to figure out what it is that he does. Not to mention that every time I see him I'm reminded of how unbelievably attractive he is. Maybe my only motive is that I just wanted to sit here and stare at him."

"Liar. Sell that crap to someone else. Tell me the truth or my car and I are outta here."

"What? He's hot!" She paused and received a look from her brother that pushed her to continue. "God, you're so difficult at times. I would totally do this with you if you asked, and I wouldn't give a rat's ass why you wanted me to."

"That's a lie too. You'd never do this in a million years with me, and you'd most likely call me creepy for wanting to do it. Enough … why are we here? What did you see? Or did you hear something?"

"Both. A few days ago I came in an hour early, and the smell of Clorox hit me in the face like nothing you've ever smelled. I dropped my things quietly and walked down to Mr. Kelley's office, peeking in to see if everything was alright." She paused and looked at Jacob and then back toward her hands, her large chestnut gaze filled with foreign emotion. "He was only in his slacks, and parts of his chest and back were covered in what looked like blood. There was blood on his floor and a bit on the walls."

"Good God, Elle. Did you call the police? Was he hurt, or did someone get hurt?"

"That's the weird part. I never saw anything but the blood and, being a bit overwhelmed by it, I simply left and called in sick that day. I wasn't sure what to do about it. I can't imagine him hurting someone, since he's such a pillar of the community and such. Besides, what if it wasn't blood, or what if he'd cut his finger or something?"

"Cut his finger? Don't you think the amount of blood or whatever would be slightly less than what you're describing from a papercut? Just because he gives to the people around him doesn't mean he's not a monster underneath all that Daddy Warbucks stuff."

She nodded and sunk down in her seat as the large figure jogged back from the house toward his car. The man stopped before getting into the back seat of the Lincoln and focusing for a minute on Jacob's car, the tilt of his head and bend of his neck telling Jacob one thing—he wasn't looking at Jacob, but at Ellie.

"We need to go," she whispered and covered her face with her small hands.

Jacob didn't wait, but put the car in drive, his eyes meeting the man's they'd come to spy on, a grimace on his mouth and anger building in his chest. If anyone made his sister feel threatened, they would be dealt with. Elle was the kindest, most pure-hearted girl he'd ever known, and the fact that she was his sister made him more than a little protective. Many of his friends had developed crushes on Ellie over the years, but Jacob never allowed anyone from the rat pack to touch his sister. She was a jewel, a treasure that only the best of the best deserved. He doubted anyone would reach the standards he'd set for his sister, but there was always hope. At least his mom thought it was possible.

Checking his rearview mirror, Jacob reached over and touched his sister's arm, his voice soft in hopes of comforting her. "He's in his car. I don't think he saw us. It's too dark out here."

*****

He'd seen them. He had to have. He was like no man Ellie had ever met, and something about him had her on edge lately. Yes, he was handsome, but the part she'd failed to tell her brother was the stark realization that she was starting to have feelings for the man she worked for. His strong, broad shoulders, short, dark hair and piercing gaze had never seemed to affect her before, but for the last few weeks he was all she could think about.

She squeezed her brother's hand and moved her arm out from under his grasp. "Thanks for coming with me. I don't know what I thought I would find. Honestly, it was just childish." She sighed softly and turned to look out the window.

"Anytime, Sis." He cleared his throat before continuing. "So, do you think the snowstorm they're predicting is going to be as bad as they say? Not like we're not used to heavy snow in the big city, but they're saying eight feet, minimum. Sounds like hell if you ask me."

Ellie laughed and turned back to her brother, reaching to turn the heat up. "They're rarely wrong. You know, they actually use scientific equipment to determine the weather. They don't have some nugget-head on the roof of a large building with his thumb in the air."

Jacob laughed and rolled his eyes at her. "Oh, they don't? And have you seen said equipment, or are you just taking for granted that they use that and not the gimp on the roof? Just because you have your masters doesn't mean you know everything."

"Yes it does." She smirked and reached for the radio, turning on the Christmas tunes.

"Oh Lord … it's not even Thanksgiving, and already this crap?"

A loud laugh followed by a snort left her as she clamped her hand over her mouth in mock embarrassment. Her brother laughed and snorted loudly, joining them together in a laughing fit.

"You're such a Grinch." She reached over and pushed at him, enjoying the light banter with her best friend. It was nice to take her mind off all the drama of the crazy theory she'd conjured up in her mind.

"Am I taking you to Mom's, or are you going back to your place?" Jacob turned down the heater and huffed a little, tugging at the neck of his sweater. "Sweating in winter … just great."

"I'm good going back to my place, sweaty. I need to think through things a little more." She nibbled at her lip, her eyes moving along the beautifully lit streets; many people in the suburbs of New York were unwilling to wait to put up their holiday decorations.

"I know you're not going to let this go, but you need to be careful, Elle." He flipped his blinker, slowing down to let a few small boys run across the street, their laughter penetrating the confines of the car. "You need to be smart about it. You can't just start stalking the guy and hope he doesn't notice. Maybe go into his office—when you're *sure* he isn't there—and look for any signs of a struggle or any remaining blood."

She smiled at the sound of the kids playing, wishing, as she did most days, that she was still one of them. Life had been good then, but lonely to say the least. "Are you volunteering to come with me?"

"Um, hell no. Your boss is three times bigger than me and I'm pretty buff." He growled a little, sounding like a caveman trying to find a mate.

"You mean butt?" She laughed.

"Haha … funny girl." He pulled the car up to a large row of red, brick single family homes. The lamps that lined the road gave off a historical ambience. "Actually, maybe I *should* come with you. I don't like you doing this alone."

"No, that would just look suspicious. It would be more natural for me just to snoop around when he's not around."

He sighed. "Fine, but if you hear him coming, you tuck tail and run back to your desk. Got it?"

She reached for the car handle, looking back at her brother as she opened the door. "Don't you worry, little brother, I'll be fine. And I don't need your help, so you can stay out of it. Chicken."

"Chicken?"

He laughed as she lunged at him before slipping out of his car and into the dark night, making the lovely sounds of a chicken in pure, unadulterated fear. The sound of his horn honking as he drove off gave her a sense of belonging again.

What would I ever do without you? Pain in my butt …

The silence greeted her as she walked into her house. A large, white fluff ball meowed and rubbed itself along her legs as she worked to get the door closed behind her; the cold front had utilized a strong wind to bring itself into town. She reached down and picked up her baby, kissing the side of his head and murmuring to him.

"Did you miss me, Marx? Was it a long day without Mommy?" She walked through the darkness while holding her cat to her chest, turning on lights as she made her way to the kitchen. Her home was small, the living room barely fitting a couch and TV, and the kitchen being made for one medium-sized rear to move around in it. Sundays with her mom and Jacob crowding around her were warm and full of fun, but a tight fit.

The sound of a voice caused her to jolt, scream softly and drop the cat.

"Did you find what you were looking for tonight, Ellie?"

She turned on the kitchen light, her hand shaking a little as her eyes fell upon her employer. His body was comfortably positioned in one of her small wooden chairs, his eyes questioning and yet not filled with malice. She couldn't speak for a few moments. The mere fact that he filled up the kitchen with his presence should've scared her to death, but all she could do was breathe in deeply, enjoying the dark hues of his cologne.

Play it cool … play it cool, Ellie.

"I'm not sure what you're referring to, but finding you in my kitchen is creepy." She stood shocked for a moment, her face flushing from anger at the idea of him thinking that it was okay to break into her house.

"You're angry."

"Just a little. Why would you think that breaking into my house was a good course of action?" She touched her fingers to the side of her head, trying not to enjoy the smile that lifted his lips.

"Why would you think it would be wise to trail me half the night? What if I wasn't the upstanding guy you thought me to be, or wait… perhaps you didn't think me such a good guy or you'd not be interested in watching me from the shadows."

She was pissed, but he had a point, sort of.

Ellie walked toward him, pulled out a chair and sat down a little ways from him, the small, round wooden table between them. She pinched her forefinger and thumb together in front of her face, a soft smile touching her lips as she said, "You have a point, but I'm still disturbed."

Her heart was beating painfully in her chest; the thought of dying at twenty-four was a bit overwhelming, and the truth of the matter was that her boss was probably up to something quite nefarious. She'd only given Jacob half the story. Whatever he was doing in her kitchen, he wasn't offering secrets or planning parties, but most likely giving her a stern warning.

A smile touched his beautiful mouth, and his full lips spread to show stark-white teeth, the gesture reaching his eyes and softening his expression. He laughed quietly, leaning forward to lay his leather-covered arms on the table before looking up at her, his dark green eyes full of self-assurance. "Do you find me that interesting?"

She felt the weight of his stare, a shiver starting in her stomach and rushing upward, until her arms were covered in goose pimples. "I have a few questions. I followed you, yes, but you're in my place in the dark."

He shrugged nonchalantly, "I'm not upset by your actions, though I can see how you feel about mine. I understand the situation."

"You do?" she asked, confused by his admission. Her own sense of reason was slipping from her grasp as her eyes moved toward his large hands, which were clasped together, one thumb rubbing along the other.

"I do. You have questions, so ask me." He stopped speaking and sat back, placing his hands in his lap, his dark slacks barely showing from her vantage point. He didn't seem to have a care in the world and she'd yet to ask what he was really doing here and how he'd gotten into her house when she was more than certain that she'd locked it up tight when she left with Jacob for the evening.

She swallowed hard, leaning forward and placing her arms on the table, knowing that her crimson fleece jacket looked professional and slimming on her feminine form. "What are you doing here, David?"

If he thought himself bold to be in her home uninvited, she was ten times more so for using his first name.

He'd never, ever given her his name, always referring to himself as Mr. Kelley to everyone he encountered. It took her a whole year to figure out what his first name was, and to use it was a no-no, or so she imagined. Tonight seemed to be the night to put everything out on the table, seeing that she was most likely going to die.

A smile tugged at the side of his mouth, his strong cheekbones and defined jaw leaving no question of his dominance. "I am here to give you a few of the answers you seek, but first you get to confess."

She scoffed, quickly forgetting his appeal and remembering how very dominant she herself could be. "I get to confess? What would you have me confess, exactly?"

"You know, it's not every day I have an attractive younger female following me around town as if I'm a wayward lover and she's in need of answers. What exactly did you and your male friend hope to find tonight?" His gaze moved from holding her own to traveling down the front of her body, her reaction causing his smirk to widen. "Do I make you uncomfortable, Miss Martin?"

"That *male* is my twin brother, and I was trying to figure out if you're a mass murderer." She wrapped her arms around her torso, one hand coming up to allow her to bite her fingernail. "Attractive younger woman, hmm?"

He laughed, and the sound warmed the whole room. For a moment, his overbearing disposition was discarded before he locked back into his façade, the persona that David Kelley wore in front of all who interacted with him. "Yes. You are quite attractive, but you know that."

He stood and walked toward the back door, opening it and smiling over his shoulder. "Strike one for not asking for what you wanted, Ellie. I offered and you decided not to bite." He walked out the back door as she stood, turning only to put the key back above the doorstop in the back of the house. "You should really be more conspicuous in all areas of your life, hmmm?"

She wanted to respond, but could do nothing more than stand and watch him leave. A soft sigh of frustration left her as the door closed. "So damn complex. How creepy is it that he broke in here?"

She chuckled to herself. *About as creepy as you and your little brother following him tonight.*

Chapter **Two**

"I can't come tonight, Krista. I'm working late." Ellie pulled up to the local coffee shop, her little red Beemer working hard to keep the heat running and the tires on the road.

"Come on, Ellie, when was the last time we saw a show together? You don't want to miss out just to hang out at the office."

Ellie pressed her ear to the phone and held it tightly with her shoulder pressed against it. "Hold on …"

"Ellie—"

"Yeah, hold on a sec."

She rolled the window down while the guy in the drive-thru window was in the middle of asking what she wanted, a soft wind bringing in little bits of snow to cover her long brown curls. She quickly ordered while Krista continued on with her chattering, telling Ellie all about the show's rave reviews. Krista's priorities obviously didn't include a morning coffee to get the day going.

Ellie growled into the phone to make sure her childhood friend knew her feelings. "I know it's going to be a great play, but I seriously have too much to do at Mr. Kelley's. He's going on a trip next week to present financials to one of his investo—" She paused as her friend questioned what it was that Mr. Kelley did exactly. "He has investors. I have no idea what he does. We've been over this a thousand times. Hold on. Let me get my coffee, or rather, let me call you back."

Before Krista could protest, Ellie hung up and dropped the phone in the seat next to her, relieved to be out of the direct line of attack. She'd worked for David for two years, and in all of that time, she'd stayed in the dark as to what exactly his investors invested in. Were they investing in him or a product? All she knew from his books were vague references to "Client Services Rendered." The more people questioned her about it, the more she realized how much it annoyed her not to know.

The guy at the coffee stand window was cute, his red hair a bit of a mess and his "No Shave November" declaration plain to see on his shirt and his face. He smiled and reached for her card, his eyes moving up to the sky as he spoke to her. "It will be $4.99 this morning. Looks like that weather is blowing in a few hours early, hmmm?"

She poked her head out the window, looking up at the dismal gray sky, and agreed quickly. "It's going to be pretty bad from what I heard, but looks like you're all bundled up?" She touched her face, smiling at him in reference to his beard.

He gave a hearty laugh before agreeing and disappearing into the coffee shop, the dark roasted smell of hazelnut accompanying the opening and closing of the service window. Her thoughts shifted back to the night before and how crazy it was that only one part of the evening disturbed her. She wasn't put off that David had caught her following him, or that he'd broken into her house. Not that he'd finally admitted that he could see her and that he found her attractive. Not even that he was sitting in the damn dark of her kitchen waiting like a creeper for her to get home.

"Why would he give me a strike? I'm not a child. How ridiculous was that?" She mumbled a few curse words at the wind before continuing. "'*Strike one for not asking for what you wanted, Ellie. I offered and you decided not to bite.*' What does that even mean?"

"Sounds like you've got two more tries and then, like they say in baseball … you're outta there." The clerk smiled and handed her the tall latte she'd ordered. A bit of heat reached her cheeks at the realization that he'd caught her pondering something rather personal out loud.

"Um, yeah … thanks." She laughed and drove off, rolling up the window and shaking her head at herself. "Such an idiot sometimes, Ellie."

The office was far too large for just the two of them, and really, it was usually just her there most days. She'd done an internship with Mr. Kelley between her first and second years in the MBA program at NYU, the experience gratifying and very well paid. That had been just over two years ago. She was more than pleased to accept when Mr. Kelley extended her a full-time offer upon graduation.

The starting salary had been twice as much as the offers she had received from various private firms. Without thinking too much about it, she had quickly agreed to work for the illustrious shadow of a man, and the rest was history. He was generous with her time off and never gave her any grief on the days she called in sick, whether she really was or not. The cozy little office was right in the heart of Manhattan's business district, putting the world at her fingertips, just outside her window.

She greeted Henry, the bellman, an elderly gentleman that reminded her of her grandfather, before hurrying into the warmth the building offered. There were at least fifteen floors in the old bank building. The bank had been long gone, ever since the 1920's, but the refurbished building offered many small businesses and investment brokers the chance to have a small piece of the pie while not having to break the proverbial bank to do so. She held the elevator for Mike, a handsome man about her age, his tie half done and his hair a mess as he rushed into the open door with a goofy grin on his face. She couldn't help but smile as she turned to him.

"You really should find someone that lives further away, Mike." She reached up to fix his tie, running her fingers through his hair to comb it back down a little. She wiped a bit of red lipstick off his mouth and laughed as his cheeks colored. "I know it's none of my business, but if she wasn't down the road you might actually put yourself together before rushing in here."

"Her husband showed up, Ellie. What can I say?" He wagged his eyebrows at her as the door opened to the third floor and he jogged off, waving and murmuring thank you behind him.

"Well, good Lord, and here I thought he was just in a relationship with a younger woman." She touched her forehead, closing her eyes for a minute and feeling much older than she was. It had been a really long time since she'd even been on a date, her life consumed with school and the CPA exam and then work. She walked out of the elevator as the door opened again on the fifth floor.

Mr. Kelley's office was on the north side of the building, a large penthouse-like space that allowed him a plush office and her a smaller one. There was also a kitchen, a lounge area and two bathrooms. The style was very classical-business, with dark woods decorating each room. Ellie was allowed to do whatever she desired with her office, her budget ridiculous for design and decoration. But after two years of not changing anything other than putting her degrees and certifications up on the wall, she'd settled into it too much to actually change anything. She unlocked the door and walked in, the sound of solitude rushing to greet her.

"David? You here, darling?" She walked through the lounge area, the crimson pillows accenting the brown leather couch perfectly. "You left in such a rush last night that I didn't get the chance to tell you just how good it was, love."

She laughed, knowing that no one would notice her morning routine, or the rest of her day, for that matter. She moved toward her office and glanced toward David's large, ornate door, fully expecting it to be closed, as it always was. Much to her surprise it was opened a bit, and the light leaking out into the small hallway left her feeling incredibly embarrassed. If he was here, he might have heard her being less than professional. She needed to watch her sarcasm.

"Figures," she grumbled as she walked into her office, leaving the door opened and dropping her large leather computer bag on the ground by her desk. Various stacks of papers greeted her, and the smell of cinnamon and cloves permeated the air due to the small candle she'd burnt the day before. The voicemail button on her phone flashed with anxiety, but her thoughts turned back to the open door at the end of the hall. She had to know if he was here and what he meant by *strike one*. "What an odd thing to say to a grown ass woman."

She gathered her courage, dropping her plush fleece jacket over her chair and stripping off her gloves and scarf. She knew that the white cotton dress she wore wrapped perfectly around her lithe figure, and the brown boots accenting the outfit were professional and stylish. She would never be accused of not looking good, her mother had made sure of that. Quietly she moved down the hallway, the smell of David's cologne providing her answer before the sound of his voice reached her.

"I am here, dear." He moved to stand before her as she stopped at the entrance of his office, his eyebrow raised slightly. "So, Miss Martin, you call me David last night and darling this morning. So quick to move from professional to personal, I see. You'll be one to watch out for, I think."

She took a tentative step back. His perfectly shaped physique filled up his navy suit, which looked to be perfectly tailored just for him. Her eyes strained to stay focused on his face, which was more of a chore than she was capable of without her coffee, which was chilling in the next room.

"I do apologize for that. I didn't realize you were here."

"So, you speak to me affectionately behind my back, but otherwise it's all business, hmm? Is that what you're saying, Ellie?" The way he spoke her name left her mouth dry and without response.

She just stared at him, realization dawning on her that the more she was around this man, the more she wanted to know him. So many secrets, and yet, in the time she'd worked with him, she'd learned that he was sensitive, responsible and intelligent. And beautiful. *God, is he beautiful.*

He turned and walked back into his office, the sunrise peeking through the far right windows giving him a shadow that seemed entirely too large for anyone to create. "I'm flying out to LA later tonight, and you're going with me."

She coughed, covering the choking that reared up in her throat. "I'm what?"

He turned and placed one of his hands on his desk, leaning into it a little, a smile touching his mouth. "I'm leaving for LA tonight at seven, and I've booked you a ticket to come with me."

"But … but …" She walked toward him, stopping at a comfortable distance. "But why?"

"Why did I book the ticket, or why am I going, or are you asking me why *you're* going? I'm a bit surprised to have caught you so off guard. Usually you're so quick on the comeback, Elle." He placed the other hand on his waist and tilted his head in a very casual manner, a manner that didn't fit the man she knew. "I can call you Elle, right?"

She nodded, not caring what name he assigned her. "Why am I going? I've never gone on a business trip with you before, and I'm a little taken aback by the fact that you're just now telling me I'm going. What if I had a date or if someone close to me was in the hospital?"

"You didn't answer my question." He stood up, righting himself before moving toward his desk and digging through his large, brown leather bag.

"What question?" She paused to rush back through the conversation as her eyes remained glued on him, watching his every move. She was beyond puzzled and unsure how to react, seeing that the events of the night before had yet to settle between them. Things just kept getting more and more odd. "Yes, you can call me Elle or Ellie or Miss Martin. Whatever you see fit to call me."

He looked up and winked at her. "Good. You're going with me because you wanted to know what it is that I do. I'm going to show you firsthand. You know, save you from having to drag your poor brother on any more stakeouts on my behalf."

She felt the blood drain from her face. Her fingers pressed against the space above her heart as it raced painfully. "I need a minute to think about this."

She heard him chuckle softly as she turned on her heel and left the room. What was he doing? Was he simply trying to get her away from family and friends in order to make her his next victim?

"Stop it," she hissed at herself as she walked back into her office and fell into her chair. Her fingers wrapped tightly around the warmth her coffee provided, her eyes closing as the warmth reached her lips and she took a long drink. She wanted to know what he was up to, and now she would know. Jacob was not going to like this.

She opened her eyes and took another long drink, a smile touching her mouth. There was a positive side to this as well. She would be getting away for … *how many days did he say?* Either way, she would be getting away for several days with the handsome man that had haunted her dreams and left her in constant question when in the waking world. Whatever he did for a living, he did really well, and if she ever wanted to move past being his accountant and get more involved in the company, something she'd always hoped for, she'd need to understand the core business.

A trip with David Kelley. All alone with him in a hotel, at dinner, at events … She closed her eyes again and let every fairy-tale moment she'd imagined over the last two years race through the recesses of her mind, a large smile touching her mouth as she realized that this was going to be a grand opportunity for several reasons. She'd put to bed the questions she had and get to know David better. And who knew what might blossom out of the trip?

"Does that smile mean you're not going to force me to make you come with me?" His voice shocked her, but the fact that he'd been watching her disjointed her even more.

"You would force me to come if I said I couldn't go?"

"Do you have a date or someone in the hospital?"

"No, but I could have." She stood up, placing the coffee on the desk beside her.

"But you don't, so it's settled. Work on the financials for Mr. Kepener until lunch and then get out of here and go get your bags together. My driver will pick you up at five, and I'll meet you at the airport." He leaned against the doorjamb, his hands tucked into the pockets of his slacks, the picture of male perfection.

"How many days will we be gone so that I know how much to pack and what to tell my family?"

He looked at his watch and seemed to be contemplating her question. "It's Thursday, so let's plan on flying back home on Tuesday next week. We'll be working over the weekend, taking a few clients to dinner and the opera and such. See you later tonight, Miss Martin. Don't be late, please."

She stood. "Wait. Do I need to pack the Kepener financials for our trip?"

"No. Everything we need, I will have with me. Just mail the old goat his financial package for this quarter on your way out." He turned to go before looking back. "Oh, and bring a few party dresses. If you have none, then I'll send you to the mall when we get settled in LA."

She closed her mouth, quite aware of it hanging open from the oddity of the conversation they'd just shared. Never in a million years would she have expected anything that had occurred over the last twenty-four hours. Shock would be a mild understatement when describing how she felt now, but instead of focusing on that, she did what she did best—got busy wrapping things up and working hard to meet deadlines that were impossible and yet pushed her to be better than the rest. Ellie Martin, the best.

Chapter **Three**

"What the hell do you mean you're going to LA with Mr. Kills-a-lot? No, you're not, Elle. It's simple, really, I refuse to let you go!" Jacob's voice rarely rose where Ellie was concerned, and yet he was yelling loud enough for the people across the street to hear him.

She turned to glare at him before opening the door to her house and moving to let him follow. "Stop being so loud. I don't want anyone around here in my business, and you're basically publicizing that I either have a pushy older brother or an abusive lover—which you are neither."

He huffed and moved down the hall, picking up the cat and turning to block her way. "I'm serious, Elle. This isn't funny. Your curiosity is going to get you hurt."

Ellie reached out and took the cat, sliding past her brother and dropping her bag in the living room. "So, you do think he would really be capable of hurting someone?"

"I don't know to be honest. What if it wasn't blood you saw, but something else?" Jacob threw his hands in the hair, his short brown hair making him look like a little boy throwing a fit. Ellie put the cat down and moved to stand in front of him, taking his face into her hands and staring intently into the chestnut colored eyes that matched her own.

"He can't be a murderer. I just refuse to believe that. He's mysterious and secretive, but he's my boss. If he needs me on a business trip, I'm going I guess. Besides, it could be fun and we'll be around other people the whole time." She patted his face and moved away from him.

Honestly, she wasn't sure why she was so confident that David wasn't capable of hurting someone, but she was. Something about him purred goodness over evil. Jacob was probably right to be cautious, but she couldn't help feeling that there was *some* other explanation. She didn't know what that was yet, but she trusted her instincts, and they were telling her that David wasn't a killer. Still, there was something going on with him and his company, and she needed to know what it was if she were going to continue to work for him.

"I'm serious. I'm putting my foot down." He moved behind her to the bedroom and stopped in the doorway of her closet as she began to pull various things off the rack and chuck them his way.

"Throw this stuff on the bed and stop worrying about me. I'm the older sister, remember?" She dropped a few things on the ground, mumbling about never wearing these items again as he obeyed and carefully moved the thrown items to the bed.

"You're a few minutes older, and you're rather naive, Sis. What if he takes advantage of you? I mean, for heaven's sake … you'll be in a hotel together. Do you at least have your own room?"

She laughed and held up a slinky black dress, one that barely covered her. "I wish he would take advantage of me, but yes … we do have separate rooms. Stop worrying. I'm a grown ass woman."

Jacob gagged and ripped the dress from her hands, throwing it back in the closet over the top of her head.

"That's just gross, and you're not wearing anything that says, 'I'm available and willing, so come take advantage of me.'"

She placed her hands on her hips and gave him the look her mother had graced them both with far too many times. "I will wear what I want and will say with my body and my actions whatever I want. I'm just glad you've agreed to let me go." She gave him an ironic smile, knowing that she'd gotten the best of him.

She reached up and grabbed a bright orange suitcase, moving past Jacob as he mumbled confusion at agreeing with her, promising that he most certainly hadn't. She exhaled softly, placed the suitcase on the small, full-sized bed before her and looked over at her brother.

"Look, I've spent two years in a cushy job getting paid far more than my peers, and I want to know why. I'm good, yes. I'm good, but no one is this good, Jacob. My boss is into something, and I want to know what." She turned back to packing, making quick work of all of the items on the bed as her brother paced the floor beside her.

"I get it, okay? Just be careful and promise me that you'll text me, like continuously, okay?" He touched her shoulder, reaching into her suitcase to grab a pair of lacy black panties and throwing them back toward the closet as he delivered their mother's look. "Promise me you'll be safe. I'd hate for something to happen to you, and then I gotta play hero and probably kill some big Goliath dude, and we know how that might go …"

She laughed and pulled him into a tight hug. "I will text. A lot. Not continuously, but I will let you know that I'm okay and that everything is fine." She moved back a little and looked up into her brother's loving face. "I need this. I'm twenty-four and have yet to have an adventure. I need this really, really bad. I will be fine. I promise."

He dropped his head in what she thought was defeat. "Fine, but please let this be a good adventure story with lovely pictures for us to ogle over and great tales of adventure. Don't let it be something that breaks you or scars you. I couldn't handle it if *anything* happened to you, Elle."

"Lovely pictures and great tales it is." She moved to zip up the bag and bent over to kiss her kitten goodbye. "Take care of Marx and give me back those black panties. They have adventure written all over them."

He groaned and followed her out the front door, waiting until the car pulled up to walk toward his own car. "Pictures and tales, Elle, pictures and tales."

*****

Outside of slowly picking off every last remaining fingernail she had, the ride to the airport was rather uneventful and long. The driver was a large Hispanic man with great manners and even better eyelashes. Ellie was almost jealous—of the eyelashes. She looked out the window as night fell, overtaken by the beautiful lights of the city and all the entertainment one could dream of.

"I understand that I'm supposed to take you to the private entrance of the airport. Did Mr. Kelley give you the code for us to get through the security gates?" the driver asked, Ellie turning to catch his eye in the rearview mirror.

"Um … no." She shook her head as if her words weren't enough to get her meaning across. "I can try and get ahold of him if you like."

"If we want to get into the gate, then we'll need the password or a guest code of some sort."

Ellie pulled her phone from her purse. Her long legs were crossed at the ankle. She remained in the same attire that she'd had on earlier, simply because she'd been unsure of what to change into. David never mentioned what the night held, but she assumed it wouldn't just be a flight to LA and then time to hit the sheets. Certainly they would grab something to eat and he would start doling out information as he'd promised. She texted his personal number and waited a few minutes, a soft sigh from the driver alerting her to the fact that they were slowly creeping up to the gate.

"He hasn't responded, but let's see if the guard will simply let us in." She shrugged her shoulders, knowing that Mr. Kelley was a complete stickler for rules and security. No way were they getting through that gate unless he wanted them to.

"Alright, miss, but I doubt this is going to work. I've worked for Mr. Kelley for the last ten years and he's secretive, if anything." The driver rolled down the window and leaned out to speak in a friendly manner to the elderly guard who came out from a small hut into the cold night air.

"Can I help you?"

The driver's voice was kind and full of energy. "You sure can, Vernon. Mr. David Kelley asked that I bring this lovely young lady to his private hangar for a quick trip to Los Angeles."

The guard peered down, and Ellie simply waved and smiled at him, truly unsure of what to do. He smiled back, looking very much like her grandpa Joe, her mother's father. He nodded and tipped his hat toward her, bidding her good evening. Turning toward the driver, he asked the question Ellie knew both she and the driver were hoping not to get.

"What's the security password for Mr. Kelley's hangar?"

The driver chuckled and looked over his shoulder at Ellie. "Gotten the password from Mr. Kelley yet?"

"Don't you know it?" she asked, smiling at him hopefully.

"Sorry, miss, but I'm under strict orders to never give it out, *no matter what.*" He shook his head at her, apologetically.

This was ridiculous. David had obviously told the driver to pick her up and bring her here, so why wouldn't he be able to just give the password for her? She sighed. It wasn't his fault, and she certainly didn't want to get anyone in trouble.

"Perhaps I can guess it if given a hint?" She tried to give her most innocent look to both men, hoping that David would text her back and help her get through this roadblock. "I've worked for him for about two years. I should know this."

The older gentleman rubbed his hands together and lifted them to his face, blowing into them before smiling back at Ellie. "Hurry up, then. No need to bring death upon me before my time, miss."

She laughed softly and nodded in agreement. "Yes, that would be tragic."

"It's a woman's name, miss," the guard said, continuing to make his physical discomfort known, though Ellie was sure he didn't realize how dramatic he was becoming.

A woman's name? Mr. Kelley hasn't mentioned a wife or girlfriend. Hell, he hasn't mentioned having a mother.

He has a mother. Everyone has a mother.

She rolled her eyes at her internal banter and blurted out the only woman's name she was sure he knew—her own. "Ellie?"

The guard winked and gave her the thumbs-up, moving back into the little metal box and opening the large red and white gate block. The driver rolled up the window and made a shivering sound before congratulating her on getting it so quickly. To say that Ellie was stunned would be an understatement. The driver started to pull away and Ellie moved toward him quickly. "Wait."

He slammed on the brakes halfway through the entrance and turned to face her. "What?"

"Wait. I need to … just wait." She opened the door and moved out of the car into the freezing cold air; the mist of early winter rested upon her coat and hair as she jogged carefully back to the security building. The older man opened the door as she approached with a look of confusion on his aging features.

"Forget something, dear?" he asked.

Small clouds of smoke lifted from her lips as she huffed from her efforts against the cold. "I just needed to know how long the password has been Ellie." She crossed her arms and shivered, not really sure why her question should matter at all, but it did. She needed to know when her boss had changed the passcode to his private hangar to her name. Surely he had other names he could use. Perhaps it was a matter of no one knowing her because he kept his business so private. Most people probably didn't even know that he had an accountant-slash-assistant.

"It's been Ellie for as long as I've been here." He smiled and pointed back toward the car as the driver began getting out to move toward them. "I think your driver is in a hurry, dear. It's getting close to seven, and I'm pretty sure the last flights out of this hangar are around that time."

She motioned to the driver to give her just one more minute. "And how long have you been here?"

He thought for a moment and shrugged. "Oh, I guess four or five years?"

She felt her heart skip a beat. "Are you saying that Mr. Kelley's password has been Ellie for the last four or five years?"

He moved back into the hut and laughed, nodding toward her. "That's what I'm saying. Not sure why it matters to you, dear, but you'd best be off. Have a safe flight and tell Mr. Kelley that Vernon said hello."

She thanked him and moved back toward the car quickly, her mind spinning precariously. After apologizing to the driver, she sunk back into the warmth of the car, the small bits of snow melting all around her and leaving wet pockets on her outer clothing.

I've only been with the company two years. Was there another Ellie? It's not a common name, is it? Surely there must have been another Ellie. It wasn't me that he thought of four or five years ago. Four years ago would put me at… well, at… twenty and a junior in college. Surely not.

It didn't sit well with her, but before she had too much time to ponder it, the car stopped and the driver opened her door, the cold air of winter rushing in and cooling her heated skin. She moved from the car and assisted with her luggage, pulling various bits of information from her purse as two men approached her, one the pilot and one the attendant for her flight.

She finished with them and walked up the small steps that led to the belly of the plane, her mind still stuck on her recent uncovering, and her thoughts far from the present. She moved toward the two seats in the middle of the plane, both empty, which was rather disappointing. She looked back toward the pilot as she began tugging off her jacket and scarf, her long chestnut hair rolling over her shoulders.

"I thought Mr. Kelley was going to be flying with me this evening."

"He is." A voice reached her from behind, and she turned in time to look up at David as he helped her remove her coat before handing it to the pilot. "Tell James that I want a scotch on the rocks and get the lady whatever she wants."

He moved toward his seat, bending over slightly to pick up his cell phone, which he gave all of his attention for the next few minutes. He chuckled softly and looked over his shoulder at her. "You made it through the gate without my help. Impressive."

Ellie sat down in her chair and shrugged her shoulders before buckling her seatbelt. "Apparently my name is the only woman's name you know?"

His smile widened as he sat down in his own seat, his black slacks perfectly pressed, the light blue shirt pulled tight across his torso and his tie loose and almost messy. His black hair accented the deeply tanned hues of his skin, and his eyes were almost golden and filled with a sense of knowledge about things she could never fathom. "What makes you think I don't know any other women besides you, Elle?"

She laughed, loving the sound of her name on his lips more than she cared to admit—even to herself. "I was just a little surprised to find out that it was my name you used, that's all."

He leaned back and thanked James as his drink was delivered. He sat in silence as Ellie ordered a Sprite and asked for a package of peanuts or crackers, something to take the edge off her hunger. After the younger man left, she looked back over at David to see if he had a response. He smirked as he turned to face her.

"I think it's quite telling that, out of all of the women's names in the world you could choose to offer up when asked what my password might be, you choose yourself." He winked at her. "Such humility you have."

She scoffed, but didn't get a chance to retort due to his phone ringing. He checked the number, sat his drink down and unbuckled his seatbelt, getting up. "I'll be back shortly."

She watched him disappear into the back of the jet, a large curtain separating them. He heard David refer to the caller as *Richard*, but that was all she heard. She smiled kindly at the flight attendant. "James, is it?"

He nodded and handed her the Sprite, reaching over to pull a small table from the side of her chair and setting down her peanuts and crackers. "Yes, and if you need anything else, please don't hesitate to ask. We have anything you could ever want on board, so please let me know if there's anything else I can get you."

She took a tentative sip of her cold drink and looked out the window as small pieces of wind and ice began to form into snow. "Thank you. How long will the flight be, and when are we taking off?"

Just then, the pilot's voice came over the intercom to advise everyone to take their seats. The flight attendant smiled at her and moved back toward the front. "Looks like we leave now, and we're looking at three hours."

She gave her quick thanks before rummaging through her purse to send out one last text to her brother, letting him know that she was fine and on the plane. Jacob would keep her mom in the loop while she was gone so she wouldn't worry. She wanted to talk to her brother about David using her name as the passcode for his security entrance. She especially wanted to talk through how and why he would have been using it for the past four to five years.

"Could be longer. The old man said it's been that way since he's been here. What about before then?" she grumbled and snuggled down into her seat, picking up her crackers and carefully tearing the wrapping. So many questions. This trip was supposed to answer most of them, but here she sat with even more questions than before, and these bothered her just as much as the ones from earlier. Should she ask him about the password? Did he know another Ellie?

Surely not.

Chapter **Four**

Ellie had finished off the crackers and the peanuts, killed two more Sprites and pulled off her brown leather boots before David returned from the back of the cabin.

Now, she thumbed through her latest romance novel, her mind not allowing her to settle on the words before her. She barely noticed David step up beside her, but the smell of his cologne tugged at her senses. She looked over and smiled at him as he sunk down into his seat. He was more relaxed now than before the call, and she looked forward to seeing a side of him that she hadn't thought possible—one where he let his guard down in front of her.

"I see you've made yourself comfortable?" He nodded toward her long legs, crimson painted toes wiggling as they were put on display.

She nodded and reached for her coat, pulling it over the front of her body and tucking her legs up under it. The chill from outside seemed to be seeping into the inner cabin, her body suddenly craving heat.

"No reason not to get comfortable for a three hour flight, I suppose." She smiled and laid her head back on the headrest, tilting her face toward him as their eyes met. He was regal, almost fierce in a way that didn't make sense. He looked like he should be fighting villains or on the back of a horse in the middle ages. Not that he didn't look incredibly superb in a business suit, ruling the world of money, but it was obvious that this man was far more than met the eye. She just wanted to know what exactly.

"I agree with that. I think we're about halfway there now, so it shouldn't be too much longer. I have a business meeting first thing in the morning, so feel free to sleep in and just meet me at eleven for lunch in the bistro near the entrance of the hotel." He turned his attention to the papers lying on the small table before him, his large fingers wrapped around the glass of bourbon and melted ice he'd ordered over an hour ago. He took a large gulp before finishing it, a sound of appreciation leaving his lips as he began to read.

She wasn't sure whether to respond to his directives or simply listen and remain quiet. Their working relationship over the last two years had been extremely professional, and most weeks they didn't talk in person, but simply via e-mail and phone messages. She really couldn't conceive of being anyone other than herself over the next five days, but he didn't know the real her. He didn't know her at all, or at least, she didn't think he did.

The need to press him about the password rose up in her thoughts again, and she pushed it back down, pulling out her novel and murmuring, "Sure" to make certain that she responded to him. She wasn't going to get straight answers from him by simply asking questions. If it were that easy then he wouldn't have played the cat and mouse game with her. He was complex, and pulling apart the layers of who he was might take more than one business trip, but if she survived this one, she was more than willing to stay the course for the long haul.

"Ellie, wake up. We're ready to get off the plane and head toward the hotel."

Ellie opened her eyes slowly, unsure of her surroundings and the foreign voice that called to her. She yawned loudly before clamping her hand over her mouth at the sound of a masculine chuckle. David.

She busied herself with pulling her boots back into place, smoothing her hair and trying to be as graceful as possible when getting up from her seat, a small mound of cracker pieces falling all over the floor. She turned to look at David and was grateful for James's approach, taking David's attention as he gave the younger man instructions on what things to gather and where to put them. Ellie picked up the small briefcase that she also used as a purse and moved toward the open door, the icy cold wind smacking into her as the pilot smiled and offered his hand to her.

She smiled in return and took it, walking carefully down the icy steps and onto the dry ground. "Thank you. Doesn't seem to be frozen here."

"No, ma'am. It'll be somewhat cold, but you'll almost never see ice or snow down here in southern California." He moved back as Mr. Kelley walked between them, his jaw locked and his eyes on the pilot.

"We'll meet you here for takeoff on Tuesday at four sharp."

"Yes, sir." He moved back and tipped his hat toward Ellie, bidding her good night as well. David turned to her and looked her over quickly.

"James will get our bags in the car. Let's go before the wind picks up again."

She nodded in agreement and moved beside him as they walked toward the stretch limo that sat just a few feet before them. A middle-aged black male held the door to the back open, a wide smile on his handsome face. Ellie

~ 43 ~

wondered if David always had people waiting on him hand and foot.

Must be weird to live your life with people all around you who are only there because they're being paid to be. Does he have a wife? A girlfriend? Brothers or sisters? Anyone?

"Elle," he said, and she was pulled from her thoughts, realizing quickly that she was just standing at the door to the car while he waited on her.

"Sorry, lost in my thoughts." She got in, tucking her cream-colored dress underneath her and making sure to cross her legs before he climbed into the cab beside her. He sat in the middle, causing their legs to be pressed against each other. Ellie tried hard not to concentrate on the thick muscle of his thigh as it pressed against his slacks. She swallowed hard and looked out the window, feigning focusing her attention on the darkness as David barked out instructions to the driver.

Once the car was in motion he leaned back, shifting a little away from her, then laying his head back and closing his eyes with a soft sigh. "I'm surprised you haven't asked me any more questions."

She laughed softly and turned to look at him, taking advantage of the fact that his eyes were closed and memorizing his features as he lay next to her. "I'm waiting for the opportune time to strike, actually. First you were on your call on the flight, and then you became engrossed in the paper, so I figured that wasn't the right time either."

He opened his eyes and she jolted a little; they were so bright that it was almost shocking, like a glowing ember deep within his gaze. He just stared at her in the silence, while her mind ran through a thousand things to say. But her last words seemed to linger in the ether around them. It was his turn to respond.

She needed to look away, wanted to relieve herself of the heavy weight of his stare, and yet something about it made her feel seen, really seen, for the first time in her adult life. Her brother, Jacob, had always protected her from both wanted and unwanted male attention, and while she wasn't completely innocent, she hadn't dated much since college.

Not sure there was a boy on NYU's campus that could stare the way he's staring. He's so calm and collected, so sure of himself. What is he thinking when he looks at me that way? Does he think I'm beautiful? Or smart? No, I'm probably just a means to an end. I'm sure he sees me as a distraction. A silly girl.

"None of those things," he whispered, closing his eyes and leaving her with another baffled look on her face.

She wanted to ask what he meant, but couldn't get her vocal chords to work for a moment. Could he hear her thoughts? That was just ridiculous. She finally found her voice.

"None of what things?" she asked, almost afraid of the answer.

The sound of the window that separated them from the driver moving down caused her to yelp, and she reached out to grab David's arm in her small moment of fear. He reached over and placed his hand on hers, squeezing it softly and moving forward to talk with the driver about the wrong turn he'd made. David helped the man quickly find the mistake he'd made and move back on track.

He sat back and looked over at her again. "We'll be there in two to three minutes. I have a few more calls to make tonight, so we can check in and then part ways."

~ 45 ~

"None of what things, Mr. Kelley?" she asked, placing her hands in her lap and trying to put forward her professional persona in order to bring him to the table for this discussion. She needed to know if he could hear her thoughts, even if the very idea seemed crazy.

"You said that I was too busy with my call and engrossed in my papers to focus on you. I was simply saying that none of those things had my attention. I was hoping you would ask some of your questions, but all in good time, right?" He smiled and reached for his bag as the car came to a stop.

She nodded, swallowing his explanation and chiding herself for being so ridiculous. No one could hear another person's thoughts. She'd been reading too many paranormal thrillers and was getting a clear dose of what she deserved — reality. She climbed out of the car behind him as he held the door open for her. The closeness of their bodies was almost overwhelming as she stood and squeezed by him. Only her name on his lips stopped her.

"Ellie … please, call me David this weekend, hmmm?"

She tucked a piece of her dark brown hair behind her ear, averted her eyes and whispered, "Of course," before moving past him and breathing in deeply. The lights of the hotel were welcoming, and the fresh, cool winter air helped to clear her lungs and her head. She was looking forward to a hot bath. She needed time to think through whether or not she was putting a spin on every little thing he said and every little move he made simply because she was suspicious in general.

"Evening, madam." The bellman held the door as she moved into the brightly lit Plaza de Flora, the most expensive hotel in all of LA. She'd heard stories of the rich and famous staying at this hotel, but never in a million years had she expected to stay for a night, much less five nights. She felt a hand gently press on her middle back and moved forward with her host's momentum, looking over at David with questioning eyes.

He didn't pay her any attention, but moved to the check-in counter, where a lovely blonde smiled with genuine warmth as she greeted them both. David's hand left Ellie, and she felt its absence immediately. Realizing that she was thinking far too much about that loss, she excused herself while he checked them in. She moved quickly to the ladies' room just across the lobby and then headed into the expansive space and leaned against the sink, staring at a tired version of herself.

A quick turn and kneel to ensure no one was in there with her, and she was back to staring at herself, with a look that her mother would be rather proud of. "You listen here. You're here to get answers, not to fall for a man that you can't have."

Why can't I have him? He's beautiful and rich and seems to like me.

She growled at herself, hating that she wanted David to show an interest in her, and even more so, that there was no one here to berate her except the person staring back at her. "Just get your damn answers and go home. He's not going to fall for you, Ellie, and he's probably a rapist or a murderer anyhow."

She closed her eyes and let her head drop, weariness settling over her. It had been a year since her last date, and that had gone off horribly. Hoping for a romance with her illustrious boss … tragedy in the making. She could be grown up about this. She would get her answers and then decide if she could still work for him, if she could respect him, or if she needed to part ways with him and go back to being like everyone else, working sixty hours a week and getting paid for thirty.

"Why does he have to be so damn handsome?" She rolled her shoulders and walked back into the lobby with her head held high.

She met his gaze head-on and smiled to give false assurance that she was perfectly fine. Extending her hand toward him, she politely asked for her key, repeated his instructions for the morning and made her way to the elevators as he took a turn toward the hotel bar. Their parting was structured and easy, and, oh, how she wanted to be ballsy enough to go with him, but that just wasn't in the cards.

She played with the card in her hand as the elevator took its sweet time rising to the top, and she sighed with relief when it hit the eleventh floor. The hall was elaborate, and the hotel smelled like freshly washed sheets and jasmine all rolled together. She breathed in deeply while unlocking the door and pushed it open with a little more angst than she intended, the door ricocheting off the wall in the room.

"Oops," she muttered and moved into the room, reaching for the lights. A soft sound of surprise left her; vibrant colors filled a vase on the table before her. "There has to be fifty roses in that vase."

She dropped her bag as she walked toward the beautiful expression of welcome, amazed that the hotel would go so far out of its way to welcome its guests. For a moment, she hoped that the bouquet might be for her personally, from her mother or brother or David. "Don't be stupid—"

The click of the door behind her caused her to stop and turn, and she sighed with relief when she realized that the door had simply shut on its own. The mysteries that had already been presented to her had her a bit on edge, and she'd be lying if she didn't admit that she wished her brother was here to talk through everything with her. She stopped in front of the roses and leaned down to smell one, the sweet aroma of love filling her senses as she groaned into the silent room.

"So incredibly beautiful." She slipped off her light jacket and designer boots and sloughed out of her dress before deciding on a hot bubble bath. In the morning, she'd have to tell the girl at the front desk how dreamy the roses were and what a great touch they'd been.

This is what it feels like to live in luxury. She smiled as she finished undressing and slipped into the heavenly warmth of a hot bath, little rose petals lining the tub and small white candles already lit for her comfort. She sank into the water and exhaled loudly, letting her mind run through a fantastic love scene only found in the best books. The main characters were beyond entranced with one another and, of course, resembled herself and her boss.

She lay there until the water got cold, her mind finally relaxing and coaxing her aching muscles to do the same. A quick dry and large, fluffy white robe later, and she was poking at the mini-bar in the room and humming a song she'd heard on the radio that morning on her way to work. A smile touched her mouth at the remembrance of being cocky enough to talk to David in a bedroom manner as she walked into work this morning, just knowing that he wasn't there, only to find him in his office.

"Figures," she huffed and stood up, bumping the table that held the roses. A little white card hit the table and sat patiently for her attention. She tilted her head, reaching for it and wondering how she'd missed it before. "Odd."

The cream-colored paper was ornately designed, with small initials running through it as if they were hand-pressed: *D.K.*

David.

She tore the paper open quickly, like a child at Christmas, and bit into the edge of her lip to stifle a sound of surprise.

Written perfectly in his clean and crisp handwriting was a note for her:

I hired you, not because you're smart, but because you're brilliant. Because you're the door to a new beginning, not a means to any end and certainly not a distraction. You are a strong, professional woman, who could never be seen as a silly girl. And, yes, I do think you're unbelievably beautiful.

Strike two, Elle.

Chapter **Five**

Ellie approached the woman at the front desk, truly unsure of what she was going to say, but knowing that to say nothing would leave her with more questions than she was willing to deal with. After a fitful night of sleep and dreams filled with lust and terror, she was ready to start making sense of some of the odd occurrences that had seemed to swim precariously around her as of late. She stopped at the counter and put her forearms on the cool marble. Her white, button down shirt was crisp, and she was wearing one of her favorite black pencil skirts. Black and white — colors of power that put most people in their place before she even had to utter a word.

"Yes, Miss Martin. How was your rest last night?" the girl asked, looking up from her computer and smiling brightly.

Ellie was a little caught off guard, not used to having someone know her name. She looked down to make sure she wasn't wearing a nametag before realizing how ridiculous that was. A nametag wouldn't have magically appeared on her chest. She growled at herself and focused back on the girl, giving her a look of what she hoped was confusion. "How did you know my name?"

The girl's smile warmed as she chuckled. "We make it a point to know all of our guests' names, Miss Martin. It's part of the deal when you stay with Plaza de Flora."

"Well, then, I'll take that deal." She smiled and laughed with the girl, her shoulders relaxing just a little as she realized that Mr. Kelley was most likely gone, seeing that it was half past eight. "I do have a question for you."

"Shoot away," the girl replied.

"I had an incredible bouquet of flowers in my room last night. I mean, there must have been fifty of them there. Do you, by chance, have any record of who might have delivered them or when they were ordered?" She feigned innocence while trying to press a dreamy look onto her face.

The girl's smile brightened. "Sure. Let me check with our concierge and I'll let you know. It shouldn't take more than a few minutes."

Ellie gave a non-verbal sign of appreciation and moved from the counter, walking toward the large glass windows that gave everyone a view of the outside world while surrounding them in rich comfort. The streets were clean, and people bustled about, trying to look important and like they had places to go. Ellie leaned against the window, her body welcoming the cool glass as her mind moved along all the open doorways that David had left her. The idea of "striking out" drove her mad, and while she was more than willing to figure things out, him talking to her as if she were a child ready to be put into time-out was about to come to a screeching halt.

"Strike two … ridiculous." She scowled and moved from the window, almost plowing the sweet attendant over. "Oh, I'm sorry. I was muttering to myself about a man."

The girl laughed and handed her a slip of paper. "I hope not about the one who ordered those roses for you?"

Ellie shook her head, reaching out to accept the girl's findings. "Unfortunately so. Thanks for this. It's quite appreciated."

The girl left her to herself, and Ellie began to open the white envelope, only to stop as she realized the attention she was gaining from the sounds coming from her midsection. *Two cats fighting for a mate in a back alley wouldn't make as much noise.*

Deciding to wait to read over the information she'd gleaned, Ellie made her way to the small bistro where breakfast was still being served. After getting a table for one and ordering both coffee and orange juice, she opened the letter and sat back in her chair, her eyes widening only slightly. The flowers had been ordered from Jean Pierre, a well-known florist at the edge of 5th Avenue, over two weeks ago. The order had been taken over the phone, and a Mr. David Kelley paid in advance for the gift.

"Yes, but did he write the note then?" she murmured, her cheeks heating a little as the waiter served her drinks and smiled timidly at her.

"Can I get you something to eat this morning, madam?" He moved back, and she noticed that his starched black and white tuxedo was almost too pristine for work in a restaurant.

She picked up the menu and took another glance at the special of the day before responding, "Yes, I'll take the blueberry pancakes with one piece of bacon and fruit on the side."

"Sounds great. We'll have that right out for you." He collected the menu and turned to leave.

Ellie spoke up, knowing that she might sound a little ridiculous, but needing to better understand the procedure for sending someone flowers. She'd never sent flowers to anyone. The only times she'd ever given anyone flowers at all were the handful of times that her and Jacob had gotten in trouble. And those times, they'd plucked the lovely creations from her mother's yard to leave on the kitchen table.

"You're a man," she said, looking up at the waiter.

Confusion swept across his features and he looked down at himself, as if checking to make sure. "Ummm. Yes."

"And men buy flowers for women, or at least most do." She sat back, a bit lost in her own thoughts, but needing to talk them out with someone. Seeing that Jacob wasn't available, this handsome waiter (whose name was *Mark*, according to his nametag) would have to do.

"That is true. Sometimes … for a girlfriend or a wife. Sometimes for a mother or grandmother." He stumbled along his words, and Ellie realized how awkward this must be for him, so she smiled warmly and laughed a little.

"Sorry. I'm trying to put together a puzzle in my head. Tell me—as I've never ordered flowers for anyone—if I wanted to buy you roses—"

He cut her off. "If you wanted to buy me roses?"

She laughed and nodded. "Yes. Hypothetically speaking. I'm a man, and you're a woman, and I want to buy you roses."

This time he laughed. "Now I'm a woman?"

She shook her head, giving him a big-sister type look. "Stay with me here, Mark. I want to buy you roses, and I go to best rose place in town."

"They're called florists, miss."

"Okay, so I go to the best florist in town, and I order roses to be delivered in two weeks to you. The question I have is about the little card."

"The little card? The one you sign with your message?"

"Exactly!" She spoke a little too loud, jumping a bit in her seat from the excitement of finally getting somewhere with the handsome, if somewhat confused, waiter. "Exactly. When would I fill out the card? Would I do it when I bought the roses or on the day they were delivered?"

He crossed his arms, looking up at the ceiling as if contemplating an answer or perhaps asking God why he always got the crazy guests. She smiled at the thought of the latter.

"If I write the card myself, then I would assume I'd do it when I buy the flowers, but if I give them the message over the phone then I could see it working either way." He shrugged and looked around the restaurant. "Let me get your order in, and I'll be back in a few moments if you need someone to continue kicking this around with."

She nodded and picked up a packet of sugar, dumping it in the dark brew that sat chilling before her and grumbling about how unhelpful that conversation had been. She still had no idea if David had filled out the card when he ordered the flowers or when the flowers were delivered. She needed to crack this part of the case.

The waiter returned and smiled down at her. "Wait, I think I have a better answer for you. You write the card when you order the flowers, unless you decide to change the message later." He tilted his head a little. "Why not just call the florist and ask when the guy gave them the message for the card you got?"

She tugged at the front of her white button down blouse and smirked at him as if they were old friends. "Who said I got flowers?"

~ 55 ~

He pointed to the letter in front of her, smiling flirtatiously. "That receipt from Jean Pierre's."

Ellie looked down at it and nodded. "Guilty as charged. Where is this flower shop, anyway?"

"Just around the corner. Wouldn't take you more than five minutes on foot, and the area is safe and clean."

"Thanks." She looked up at him and smiled before he walked away, and she once again became lost in her thoughts of the mysterious man she worked for. Where was he now? What was he up to? When did he write the damn message for the flowers?

"Why me?"

After gathering her lightweight jacket from the hotel room, Ellie made her exit from the hotel and slipped in amongst the innumerable people rushing down the street. *Is everyone running late for work?*

Her breakfast had been beyond perfect, and her waiter had tried his hand at flirting with her, even though she'd made it known that she'd received flowers from another man. She laughed to herself at the very thought of how arrogant guys her age and younger were. To guys like that, there was nothing better than finding a beautiful woman to show off, but it was even better if she belonged to someone else and you snagged her off his arm.

Jean Pierre's flower shop was just as close as the waiter had said, but much busier than she'd imagined. The small shop was no bigger than a coffee house, and yet there were about twenty people looking to buy the perfect flowers. Ellie made her way to the counter. A young woman, who looked to be just a few years younger than Ellie, was speaking with a customer as she wrapped a bouquet of brilliant yellow lilies.

"Yes, Mr. Parker. She's going to love these."

"Are you sure yellow is her favorite, Gen?" He tugged his jacket closer, reaching into his pocket and pulling out a rather fat wallet.

The girl laughed and nodded her head, dark eyes moving toward Ellie as she spoke. "I'll be right with you, dear." She turned back to the man before her. "I'm one hundred percent positive, Mr. Parker. I wrote it down in your file last time you and your wife were in the shop. My father knows everyone and remembers all of their favorites, rest assured."

"She's correct, Kevin," a loud, robust voice called out from behind the dark curtain in the back. A moment later, the man who owned it made himself known. Ellie assumed he was Jean, since the girl had referenced her father and this man had an air of confidence that made him seem like he owned the place.

"Then I shall take your word for it, Jean." The customer smiled, paid and picked up his flowers, turning toward Ellie and smiling as he moved past her.

She moved toward the counter as the girl grumbled softly about the man taking her father's word, but not hers. She looked up at Ellie and huffed, a long dark strand of hair flying about her face.

"Men." She smiled as Jean moved back behind the curtain again. "What can I do for you? Thank you for waiting."

Ellie nodded, setting her bag on the counter and looking around at the beauty that filled each nook and cranny of the room. "Men indeed," she muttered and looked back at the girl in time to share a quick laugh.

"I actually got the most beautiful roses in the world last night, and the card came from this shop." Ellie placed her hands on the cold glass counter between them and continued. "The card said that they were from my boss, a Mr. David Kelley, but I wanted to know when he filled out the card that went with them."

The young girl smiled and placed her hands on her hips. "I see. You're sleuthing."

"Is it that obvious?" Ellie laughed softly and reached up to tuck a piece of her own dark hair back into place.

"You'd be surprised how many people we have coming in asking questions about the flowers they received … or didn't receive." She laughed as Jean walked back out, a smile on his handsome face, his head so shiny and bald that the light reflected off his skull a little.

"And Mr. Kelley is very particular about who he sends flowers to," the owner of the shop said softly, the timbre of his voice welcoming and fatherly.

"Oh, you know David?" Ellie asked, her curiosity piqued.

"I know of him, dear. Not many people know Mr. Kelley, but we all know of him. He's quite a pillar of our community. But your question is about the flowers you received and not necessarily about the man who sent them, correct? I mean, if you work for him, as you say you do, then obviously you know him much better than I, right?"

She almost enjoyed the rabbit hole the florist created as he weaved words around her. They were nearly as intriguing as the various flower arrangements that filled the air with their perfume. She nodded and pulled the white piece of paper from her bag. "I know the order was put in two weeks ago, but what I need to know is if he called to change the message on the card last night."

Jean's eyes bored into her, not in an uncomfortable manner, but more as if he were trying to figure her out. His face softened as his daughter reached over and touched his arm gently, her voice quiet in order to keep the conversation between the three of them. "I'll grab the record book from the back. There's no harm in answering her question, Papa."

He looked at his daughter and then back toward Ellie and nodded. "Gen is right. I will let her look for you, and if you need anything else, just give me a holler." He moved from the counter, his voice filling up the small space as he greeted various customers by name. Ellie sunk down a little where she stood, a small sigh of relief leaving her lips as the girl disappeared behind the curtain. She had a million more questions to ask, but Jean had made it clear that flowers were the only thing he was going to talk about when it came to Mr. Kelley.

Everyone knows of him but people don't know him? Pillar of the community? In LA?

That would explain why he's gone all of the time. He could be here, living another life—or, really, just living life. It's not like he's ever in New York, right?

"Okay, let's take a look." The young girl pulled open a large book and leaned over the cream-colored pages, her small finger trailing down the page as she mumbled through the names she read. "David Kelley, here we go."

Ellie leaned over to see that he had ordered the flowers two weeks before, just as the hotel clerk had said. There didn't seem to be any additional markings or notes, but

Ellie wasn't sure of the flower shop policies, so she stepped back to let the girl look and patiently waited for a reply.

"Nope, I'm not seeing any adjustments, so he placed the order two weeks ago and gave us the message for the card then." She looked up at Ellie and smiled kindly. "Does that help?"

Ellie touched her mouth, pondering this. "Do you know what message he wrote?"

The girl's eyebrow lifted. "Don't you know the message he wrote? You got the flowers, right? The delivery went well last night?" She almost looked concerned, and Ellie reached out and touched the table between them, her face softening.

"Oh yes. The order was there last night, and the flowers were beautiful." *How am I supposed to ask this without sounding crazy?* "The message was a little odd, so I just wanted to check to see if what he originally sent over to you was what I received. I might have upset him, and if so, I figured I could tell by seeing if the message had changed since the order was originally placed."

The girl nodded, looking at the book again before turning it fully around for Ellie to see. Her small finger moved along the page as Ellie's eye caught up. "Here's the message he gave us."

Ellie's eyes finally found the small scribbled handwriting and focused on what she already knew would be there.

I hired you, not because you're smart, but because you're brilliant. Because you're the door to a new beginning, not a means to any end and certainly not a distraction. You

*are a strong, professional woman, who could never be seen as
a silly girl. And, yes, I do think you're unbelievably beautiful.*

Strike two, Elle.

She stepped back from the book and picked up her
bag, looking up at Gen. "That's the message I got, too."

"Well, it's a beautiful one. Seems that your boss
might have feelings for you. It's too lovely not to notice the
underlying message, hmmm?"

Ellie's laugh was soft and fell flat; a small flame of
fear curdled with hope threatened to cause her stomach to
turn. "Thank you for your time today. You've been most
helpful. And if Mr. Kelley asks, for some strange reason, I
was never here."

The girl nodded. "Was there anything else I could
help you with?"

Ellie smiled and shook her head. "No, but thank you
for offering." She turned and walked from the shop. As she
stepped outside, the wind wrapped around her and blew her
long, silky brown locks about. At a time like this, when
nothing made sense, she figured she would do what she
always did. She pulled out her cell phone and slipped into a
small coffee shop just beside the flower shop, the smell of
warm roasted coffee filling her senses and offering comfort
that didn't make much sense.

"Jacob," she said breathily into the phone. "I just
needed to hear your voice. You got a minute, or an hour or a
day?" She laughed and sank down into a booth, spilling her
guts to her brother while trying not to give him too much to
worry about. But based on the sharp sound of his questions

and comments, calling him might not have been her best move.

Just before wrapping up her call with Jacob, the soft touch of a hand on her shoulder pulled her attention. She looked up to see Mr. Kelley looking down at her. Even with all of her questions, his gaze was comforting in this city where she knew no one, and his smile was welcomed.

"Alright, well, I'll call you tonight. Hope your day goes great, and tell Mom I love her." She didn't wait for her brother to respond, but hung up and pointed to the chair across from her. "Mr. Kelley, please, join me if you'd like."

He looked over at the barista taking orders and back at Ellie. "Who comes into a coffee shop and doesn't order coffee? What do you want? I'll grab us something warm."

She laughed, realizing how ridiculous she must've looked, but her appearance hadn't been at the forefront of her thoughts as she'd piled into the small shop, her mind buzzing and her heart racing. "I'll take a vanilla latte with fat free milk."

He nodded and walked away, his hand squeezing her shoulder softly before doing so. In all the years she'd worked for him they'd barely made physical contact, and yet, in the last two days, he'd touched her more than a few times. She let out a shaky breath and texted her brother the reason for the abrupt hang up, hoping that would suffice until she could have a more elongated conversation with him. She closed her eyes and let her head drop back just a little, all of the questions she had for David rushing through her mind, and each begging to be selected first.

"Did you like the flowers, Elle?" he asked as he sat down and slid the drink toward her, a smile on his ruggedly handsome face. He filled out his pin-striped suit perfectly.

She took the drink, her eyes never leaving his as she nodded. "I loved them. It was the card that gave me a bit of heartburn. Care to explain?"

His eyebrow lifted, and a smirk played along his mouth, his body visibly relaxing as he took a tentative sip of his dark liquid. "Card? What did it say, exactly?"

She laughed, setting down the cup and leaning forward with a bit more confidence than she felt. "Strike two. Am I getting one more and then I'm out?"

He sat down his cup and leaned toward her. His fingers touched a long strand of her hair softly before he let his eyes settle back on her. "No, Elle. One more strike and you're in. As far as how deep you really want to go, but that part I'll leave up to you."

Chapter **Six**

Ellie had no idea how to respond to his words or his closeness. The intimacy with which he spoke caused her stomach and chest to tighten in anticipation of something to come, and yet fear played around the edges of her emotions as well. Nothing ever worked out well for her in the relationship department, and he was obviously talking about her learning about his work, not about her getting in deep ... with him.

"I assume that the hotel was to your liking? Sleep well last night and all?" He leaned back languidly, the man all too comfortable in his own skin.

"Yes, it's great. I wasn't sure what to expect, but it's beyond anything I could imagine." She picked up her cup, trying hard to focus on breathing at a normal rate and not panting like some lovesick fool. She took a sip and smiled as the flavors of comfort rushed across her tongue.

"Good. I'm glad you're pleased. Tonight we'll be attending a dinner party of sorts, a black tie affair, if you will. If you don't have something suitable to wear, make sure that you go shopping this afternoon. You and I will talk business with a few of my clients tomorrow, but in the afternoon, I have a few personal matters to attend to. You still have your business Visa, correct?"

She nodded, taking another sip of coffee before answering. "Yes, and I guess that settles where I'll spend my afternoon. I mean, I brought mostly business attire and a dress or two for a casual dinner, but nothing for the type of event you're talking about."

He smiled, his fingers rubbing along the small espresso cup as his eyes lingered on her. "I'm sure you'll find something that looks stunning."

She blushed and shook her head. "Are you always so complimentary? I find it almost charming, and yet I didn't know this side of you existed. You travel all the time, and I've realized that we barely know each other."

"Should we?" He spoke softly, the strong features of his handsome face perfect in structure, as if carved from marble.

"Should we what, Mr. Kelley?"

"Please, call me David." He picked up the cup and took a tentative drink as the door to the shop opened and a gust of wind blew a nearby paper onto the floor next to them. He bent over to pick it up and then looked back at Ellie. "Should we know one another?"

She wasn't sure how to respond and was grateful that she didn't have to. A large, boisterous red-haired woman walked toward them from the doorway to the shop, a smile on her face and joy written across her features. "Well, look who the cat dragged in!"

David stood and smiled warmly. Ellie was almost surprised that someone with David's demeanor would know, and even be friends with, such an extrovert. He extended his hands toward the woman, and she placed her hands in his and leaned in for a kiss on each of his cheeks, her bright blue eyes searching Ellie as she looked down toward her.

"Sandra Barker. So nice to see you again." David moved back and motioned toward Ellie. "This is my assistant and my accountant, Ellie Martin. Ellie, this is Ms. Barker."

Ellie stood, carefully placing the white napkin from her lap on the table before her and extending her hand to the older woman. "Very nice to meet you, Ms. Barker."

"You likewise, child." She shook Ellie's hand quickly and turned her attention back to David, her smile widening almost too much. Ellie bit at her lip to stifle a smile and sat down, grabbing her coffee cup and feigning interest in the caramel-colored liquid.

"Please, do tell me you'll be at the gala tonight, Sandra?" David spoke as if they were old friends, and though she hated herself for it, Ellie felt a bit of jealousy sweep across her. David was probably somewhere in his mid-thirties, which made her feel a bit young for him. But, this lady had to be at least in her late forties if not early fifties, and not his type at all, at least not what Ellie would assume to be his type.

And what type would that be? I've never seen him with a woman before. Guess I'd just like to imagine that his type is someone like me.

Dream on…

"Of course I will be. You got your invitation, I pray?" She reached out and pawed at his chest a little. He captured her hand and kissed her knuckles, the woman's cheeks coloring to match her wild looking hair.

"I did, and Ellie and I will be in attendance. Black tie, I assume?" He smirked a little as Sandra turned her attention to Ellie, the look on her portly face almost showing disappointment.

"It is black tie," she said with a clipped tone before looking back toward David. Her tone of voice shifted quite dramatically when she added, "It's a masquerade ball, though, so make sure you and your secretary get a mask, or you'll be given one at the door, and the ones they hand out are just ghastly!"

Ellie noticed that the rest of the patrons in the coffee shop were sneaking glances in their direction; the woman's voice was so thick and full of excitement that it was hard to ignore her.

"Sounds perfect. We'll get ourselves masks for the event. And Ellie is my accountant, not my secretary," he chided her playfully.

She just giggled and asked him to save her a dance. He promised he would and sat back down as she walked off, his eyes locking onto Ellie's.

"That was … interesting." Ellie tried to break the ice without asking too much or giving away her impression of David's admirer.

"Yes, well most of the people you meet tonight will be in full effect. They all live in LA for a reason."

"And that reason is?" Ellie took the last sip of her coffee before sitting back and enjoying the view of the dark-haired, mysterious male before her.

"Namely because it's the only place they can fit in and be who they are without being arrested." He chuckled and soft smile lines formed along the edges of his eyes. "So, we have another thing to add to your shopping list."

"Yes. Masks, check. Do you need me to get you one as well?" she asked, wondering where in the world she could get a mask from and what type of mask she would get someone of David's stature and character.

"If you're asking me if I have a mask in my suitcase, I think I'll just let the question die between us."

"Why's that, Mr. Kelley?"

"It's David, and I think it would be more fun to let you think I don't and then be surprised if I do." He smiled with what appeared to be nefarious intent, and her heart fluttered. He was beyond dangerous, and if there was an exit sign telling her where to get off the road to pure destruction at the hands of this man, she'd missed it or burnt it down in her sleep. She wanted to know everything about him, but mostly she wanted to understand what made him tick.

He stood, picking up his briefcase. "I'll meet you at six sharp in the hotel lobby. Be dressed to go and feel free to spend whatever you need to on your outfit, hair, nails, and anything else for tonight. Just don't forget to grab me a mask along with yours. Use a driver from the hotel and be safe."

She called after him as he turned to go, "What kind of mask should I get you?"

He smiled over his shoulder. "You know me better than you think you do, Elle. Pick something out that you think fits me, and I'm sure it will do just fine."

She chuckled at her thoughts of what type of mask might fit someone who was so rugged and handsome, so commanding and smooth. Nothing could make his face appear more intriguing, but she'd do her best. Her goal wasn't going to be to make him more attractive, but to make herself so stunning that she'd leave him breathless.

She grabbed her things and rushed from the coffee shop, realizing that she'd need the full afternoon to find a dress and heels, have her hair and makeup done and be ready for him by six tonight. Excitement tore at her nerves as she moved quickly among the lunch crowd, her smile contagious to the people around her.

The rest of the afternoon was spent running at a pace that honestly exhausted her. A nap was in order, and yet she still had a hair and makeup appointment and definitely needed to shave her legs. Having someone trip over her leg hair that evening would be less than brilliant, and she'd be forced to tell her brother, who would then make fun of her for eternity. She smiled at her ridiculous thoughts and tucked the edge of her white terrycloth towel a little tighter around her bosom.

Humming the latest boy band song to herself, she made her way to the bathroom to wrap up her portion of the appearance overhaul, leaving a full length velvet dress fanned out on the bed. It had fit her like a glove, the off-the-shoulder dress hugging just above her breasts tightly and accentuating the small amount of cleavage she had. The split up the right thigh was a little dramatic, but hopefully the room would be dark and there would be so many people crowded around that it wouldn't be too terribly noticeable.

She'd done herself some good by bringing a few pieces of jewelry; one of her gold necklaces coordinated with the dress perfectly, lying just above the neckline. With her hair straightened and then given a heavy, old-fashioned curl, she'd be the belle of the ball, or something like that. A laugh resounded around her and she realized how incredibly giddy she was about the whole thing.

"This is ridiculous. It's just a gala and he's my boss." She sat on the edge of the tub and started to shave meticulously, taking her time so she didn't cause any nicks on her most valuable asset. "You're here to see what he does and determine if he's a mass murderer or a vampire."

She stopped and laughed loudly at the thought of him being a vampire. That would be wicked hot and scary as hell. She needed to lay off the paranormal romance reading late at night. It was doing nothing to add to her mental stability. David was most likely just a stockbroker that traveled a lot and hadn't found the right woman to settle down with. Not that Ellie assumed she was that woman, but it wouldn't hurt at all to have a few candlelit dinners with him, dance to slow music, drink some wine and … and well, who knew what else? She sighed loudly, trying to remove him from her thoughts altogether. Being rather unsuccessful, she hurried through the rest of her duties and left the bathroom a hairy mess.

The phone pulled her from her thoughts, and she rushed around the room, trying to throw on a t-shirt and shorts, as if someone were at the door instead. She stopped at the phone and calmed herself before answering it like she would at work. "This is Ellie."

"Hi, Miss Martin. This is Eric from the front desk. We were told that you needed a driver to take you to La Champarian's to get your hair done for the evening? It is nearing two-thirty now, and I believe you informed us that you'd need to be there at three. We'll need to get going soon if that is the case."

"Oh, yes. Thank you so much. I'll be down shortly." Ellie hung up and dropped to the bed nearest her, trying to still her heart and reason with herself that this event wasn't really that big of a deal. The only problem was—it was. The last time she'd found a reason to get all dressed up was a high school dance that had gone rather poorly; her date had left her on the dance floor and she had spilled an entire bowl of red punch on her brother's pants. She smiled in remembrance before moving around the room to dress herself in jeans and a sweater. She pulled on her boots, grabbed her jacket and purse and ran out the door with cell phone in hand.

After texting Jacob that she was good and would call later that evening, she made her way down to the lobby and stopped at the front desk, locating the attendant whose nametag defined him as Eric.

"Hi. I'm Ellie. You called up and said my driver was available now?"

He smiled and pushed a button on the counter before him. "He sure is. Have a great time, and make sure when they ask what you'd like to drink, you tell them the green dragon."

She laughed, raising her eyebrow slightly. "The green dragon?"

He pointed behind him to her driver, who was holding the door of the hotel open for her. "Yes, you won't be disappointed. It's quite a treat. Have a great time, Miss Martin, and we'll see you shortly."

She shook her head. Her long, dark-brown hair was still a little damp from her shower earlier. She reached up and rolled it into a tight bun as she walked toward the open door and greeted her driver. She hadn't seen him before, but she assumed the driver was employed by the hotel and not by Mr. Kelley. That would just be a little much. The man was wealthy, but to have a driver in multiple cities seemed excessive.

To say they treated people like royalty at La Champarian's would be a mild understatement. After being handed a soft, silky robe and fluffy, cream-colored slippers to match it, Ellie was shuffled into a changing room and told to lock her belongings in a small locker and get ready to relax.

"I just came to get my hair done, though. Is there a mistake?" She peeked back out around the changing room door, trying to get the attention of the handsome young male who had quickly moved her to where she stood now.

"No mistake. We do not just simply do hair, miss. We are a full service salon here, so everything is included in the price you're paying today. Just change quickly and Marco will meet you at the back of the salon to start working on your hair." He paused and tilted his head a little. He had white streaks in his hair that definitely had to have been added on purpose, seeing that he couldn't be out of his twenties. "If your color were a few shades darker, you would go from beautiful to stunning. Yep, that's what we'll do."

Ellie didn't have time to respond before he left her standing there, staring after him. "Well, then. I guess that's what we'll do." She shut the door and made quick work of her clothing. Most of the time she spent in the little dressing room was debating whether she should leave her panties and bra on or take them off. *What do people do in these fancy-ass situations?*

Taking them off might make her seem loose, almost as if she'd misunderstood what full service meant. No happy ending for her there, no sir. She finally decided to stick with the underclothing and dressed in the cloud-soft robe they'd given her, then sighed contentedly as she moved toward her hairdresser for the afternoon. The rest of the appointment went like clockwork, and it was only when she was getting her toenails painted that she realized she'd forgotten to order the green dragon drink that the hotel attendant had so kindly brought to her attention.

"Oh, I meant to ask," she started, looking down at the girl that was working on her toes while talking softly about the various shops and theatres in the surrounding area.

"Yes, miss?"

"One of the guys at the hotel where I'm staying said that I absolutely had to request your green dragon?" She phrased it as more of a question, just in case there was no such thing. Saving herself from foolishness was something that she'd gotten quite good at, since she had a twin brother who couldn't help but get them both into situations that left them looking like fools.

The nail technician laughed and turned to call for the green dragon. "Good choice. Most people don't know about the drink, but someone definitely did you a favor."

Ellie sat back, relaxing a little, and continued to push the girl for information. "What exactly is in the drink?"

"It's pineapple, green apple liquor and Everclear, but it's blended with ice and a little bit of cream. It's delicious." The girl shrugged and went back to carefully painting Ellie's toes.

"It sounds great, but the guy made it sound like it had magical powers or something." She laughed softly, closing her eyes and enjoying the pampering.

"It does have a bit of a kicker in it."

Ellie's eyes opened. "What do you mean a kicker?"

"Well, the man that owns this shop has a specialty store as well, down on Broadway and Main Street, and the concoctions he brews over there are said to heal the sick and bring light to the blind." The nail technician shrugged again as if they were simply talking about the color of their socks.

"And people really believe that?"

"Oh yeah. We've seen it happen." The girl turned to take the drink from the African American man who had brought it and handed it to Ellie. "He puts a small drop of magic into each of these drinks. Not many people know to ask for them, and even when they do, they just think they're hallucinating a little after drinking it, I suppose. That's what I thought until I began to understand who my boss is."

Ellie tentatively took the glass, not willing to accept anything the girl was saying, and yet wanting to push the conversation, simply because she was curious. "And this magic … what exactly does it do?"

"Well, it takes a few hours, but all it does is open your eyes." She moved back and smiled. "Your toes look perfect. Do you like them?"

Ellie looked down and nodded, lifting the drink to her lips and taking a small sip, the tropical flavor rushing across her tongue and beckoning her to drink it down. She took a longer sip and gave a small sound of appreciation. "The toes look great and this drink is wicked good."

"I'm glad you approve. I think we're done, so if you want to move over to the dryer we'll just put your feet under there, and then you're ready to check out." The girl helped Ellie up and moved with her to the dryer.

"What do you mean, the magic opens my eyes? My eyes are already opened." Ellie chuckled a little, as if she were just teasing the girl.

"Your eyes are open to what you've been taught to see, but there is so much more going on around us that we don't even know."

"And this magic in my drink will show me that?"

"Absolutely." The girl spoke with calm conviction, as if this were no big deal. Ellie sat back, a bit dumbfounded, but unable to remove her lips from the small, coconut-flavored straw as she drank deeply, another song running through her mind and relaxation setting in deeply. Magic was exactly what she needed to get through this night. A room full of strangers, and the most complex person of all was her date.

Chapter **Seven**

"What do you mean, he wants me to meet him there?" Ellie huffed into the phone. The poor attendant on the other end tried to offer her comfort, but it wasn't really his place to do it. David was supposed to pick her up so that they could attend the gala together, and now, because of business, he would have to meet her there. She spoke with the clerk for a few more minutes, then got off the phone, hoping that someone at the front desk would know where this event was taking place.

"Figures," she mumbled into her empty room and finished putting herself together before stopping by the bathroom to make sure she looked as decent. The long, velvet black gown looked as if it were custom made for her, accenting the thick fullness of her soft, dark-brown curls. Her makeup was a little darker than she'd usually wear it, but having her face hidden behind a mask all night made that necessary.

"Shit!" She shook her head and rushed out of the bathroom. "I knew I was forgetting something. The freaking masks. There has to be a place to stop between here and the gala."

Grabbing the new black leather jacket she'd picked up, she placed her purse over her shoulder and made her way down to the lobby. The driver she'd had earlier hurried forward to greet her and opened the door, a smile on his face. "Miss Martin. Right this way."

"Thank you. I sure do hope you know where we're going, because my date is running late and meeting me there, wherever 'there' is." She shrugged and climbed into the back seat of the stretch limo, realizing that she'd quickly become accustomed to the idea of being wealthy and waited on hand and foot.

He slipped into his seat as well, readjusted his mirror and chuckled. "Mr. Kelley gave me the location of the gala, so worry not. He always takes care of every small detail."

She shook her head, smoothing down her dress and trying to follow his instructions to not worry. "Yes, well, I wish he would've picked up our masks for this thing. I completely forgot, in all of the hustle and bustle, to do so. Is there somewhere we can stop on the way?"

A small red and bright pink bag was extended toward her from the front seat, and Ellie reached up to take it and review its contents. Two masks sat in the bag, dark shimmery paper framing them. They were beautiful. Hers was feathered and dark, with accents of crimson and gold, and his was gold and black.

"Wow," was all she could say as she carefully touched the gift. The car pulled out into traffic, and she settled back in her seat, feeling shocked and maybe a little paranoid. How could David have known that she wouldn't have time to pick up the masks? Was someone following her? Did he have a chip in her arm that she didn't know about?

Now I'm just being ridiculous. At least, I think I am.

Her phone buzzed in her small purse and she pulled it out, thankful for the interruption from the incessant questions that circled through her skull at an alarming pace.

What was the deal with that drink today?

Who was the owner of the salon and the specialty shop that the nail technician had mentioned?

How did David know she'd be at the coffee shop?

How the hell did he write that note two weeks ago when it perfectly answered her thoughts from the night before?

Why, how, what? What about the blood?

"Hello," she answered her phone and sighed in relief to hear her brother's voice.

"Hey, Sis. Having that adventure yet?" Her brother sounded like he'd had a beer or two, or three.

"Sort of. What are you up to? Mom okay?"

"Yeah, she's fine. I wanted to tell you about something I found out regarding your mystery man."

She laughed. "My boss."

"Yeah, him too. Look I couldn't help but try and dig up a little information on him. You know my good friend Jimmy from the IRS? Well, I had him look into Mr. Rich-britches."

She felt almost ashamed for wanting to know. "And? He should be fine as far as money and taxes go. I'm his damn accountant, Jacob."

Her brother laughed, and she couldn't help but smile as well. "Nothing came up there, so I started digging on my own, and you know what I found?"

"What?" Her eyes moved to focus just outside the window as the scenery changed from large buildings glowing with light to a more residential area, with houses as large as some malls.

"He has no family that I can tell. No brothers or sisters, no record of a mother or wife. Nothing."

"That's ridiculous. Everyone has a mother. What about his father." She realized what she was saying. "Wait …

~ 79 ~

stop looking into him. I don't want him to know we're sleuthing around. I just want to know what he does for a living. Hell, what I do for a living."

"He already knows we're sleuthing around, and I did find something on his father."

"What?" She was almost annoyed at herself for her sudden mood swings. She'd gone from wanting to know nothing, to needing to know everything, to honestly just being disgusted with herself. People didn't investigate other people like this. Maybe if he were her fiancé or something, and she thought he might be cheating, then there would be a damn good reason for looking into him, but simply to find out where her boss made his money? Ridiculous.

"His father died twenty years ago and left everything to him."

"Most dads do that, Jacob."

"Not ours, thank you very much," her brother said, scoffing.

"We didn't know our deadbeat dad. Anyway, you never know, maybe when he dies some lawyer will come out of the woodwork and give us the keys to the kingdom." She scooted toward the window and pressed her forehead against it, wishing she could just forget about all of this.

"Don't hold your breath. However, the weird thing about his father is that he looks just like him, Elle."

She moved back from the glass as the car came to a stop in front of an enormous white house; the President's mansion in DC had nothing on this place. "Most boys resemble their fathers, Jacob. This is stupid. Why did you call, you silly goof? If you were worried, then just say that and don't be all cryptic, making me think you found something when you didn't."

"No!" Her brother's voice changed a little, moving from jovial to serious. "He looks *exactly* like his father, like the spitting image. He even has this small scar on top of his left eyebrow, Sis."

"I'm getting off the phone. I'm at a gala event that I have to go look beautiful for. I'm sure it's just a coincidence. Besides, I'm sure if we ever saw our dad you'd look just like him too, silly."

"Fine, but his grandfather and great-grandfather both have it too."

"You looked back that far?" She moved back to let the driver open the door.

"Yes, and one thing I know for sure, Elle, is that scars aren't hereditary, at least not the physical ones."

"Miss Martin, so nice to have you join us tonight." The dark-haired gentleman at the door moved behind her and helped her slide out of her leather jacket, taking her purse as well.

Ellie pulled the masks from the small shopping bag she'd been given and handed the bag off to the man as well. "How did you know my name already?"

He smiled warmly and she couldn't help but relax a little. Perhaps the night wouldn't be so bad after all. The key was to find David and stick by his side. These were his clients—and hers, to some extent—but she had no idea who they were or what sorts of things David was investing in for them. If he'd sold something physical she could dig deeper, but having his services revenue simply labeled "Client Services" in the books gave her nothing. She huffed softly and turned her attention back to the man.

"David's had you listed as his assistant and accountant for the last two years, Miss Miller. Your picture is usually next to his in his portfolio presentations and such." He nodded toward the opening at the end of a large, ornate hall. "Please, do make yourself at home. The cocktails are being served for the next hour or so, and then we will have a plated dinner. David is already here, so I'm sure you'll see him when you enter the room to the left."

She smiled, feeling a bit of excitement course through her. The conversation with her brother sat oddly in her thoughts, but she knew it would take a quiet room and some time to really think to work through whether any of Jacob's concerns and claims were valid. Lots of people looked like a member of their family. That didn't necessarily mean anything.

She thanked the helpful gentleman and walked toward the room he had pointed out to her. Music emanated from the room, filling the air with a soft and steady beat.

The house was decorated in a traditional style; the pictures on the walls were formal portraits. Everything felt so proper, and yet she felt like she fit in perfectly. Most of the men that moved about the room were in full tuxedos, and the women were in everything from cocktail dresses to elaborate ball gowns. She held her mask up to her face, the dainty little thing only covering the area around her eyes, almost giving her a cat-like appearance, she imagined. David's mask hung in her hand, and she rolled the long velvety stick that held it together around and around in her fingers.

She moved toward the large bar, which ran the length of the room. The rest of the space before her was filled with large chairs and couches, all made of leather. The smell of sweet cigar smoke lifted in clouds around her, and the regality of the room was almost suffocating. She stopped by the bar and pulled her mask down to speak to the male bartender, his long blond hair touching his shoulders as he looked up and smiled.

"Can I have a gin and tonic, please, sir?" She smiled, enjoying the attention as his eyes roamed over her, then wondering if she'd be so quick to search out the attention of another if David were here to see. *It's not like we're together. Ridiculous.*

"You know," — the soft touch of someone's breath brushed across her exposed left shoulder, the strong press of someone's chest against her back — "you're supposed to keep your mask on at all times during the night. It adds to the allure, suggesting that you aren't exactly who you say you are, Miss Miller."

She turned her head slightly, a smile touching her mouth as she looked at her boss's profile, his head bent, lips so close to her shoulder. "Then you shall need this, I suppose, to keep up pretenses, yes?" She reached across the front of her body and handed him the mask he'd given her to bring for him.

Returning her attention to the bartender for a moment, she reached out and took the drink, thanking him and then turning to face David. "I thought you were going to come by the hotel and pick me up, but you keep requiring me to prove to myself that I can traverse this city alone. Or am I proving that to you?"

He looked up at her, and she felt her breath catch in her chest; she swore she saw the air shimmering a little as he spoke to her. "I don't think you have anything to prove, but if you feel otherwise, I'm obliged to allow you to be only who you are."

~ 83 ~

She smiled and moved back a little, her fingers brushing her hair back as she felt faint for some reason. Perhaps because of the closeness of this exquisite man. Closing her eyes for a moment, she breathed in and could swear she could taste the sweetness of the mint on his breath. She opened her eyes and reached for him as the room spun slightly.

"Everything okay, Ellie?" He spoke quietly, moving in to hold her up by the back of her arms. She nodded and smiled, trying to shove off the feeling that the room had suddenly become illuminated and the colors were more defined. The darkness of David's eyes had become the darkest shade of jade she'd ever witnessed, and the colors of his skin had moved from the normal hues of life to something almost luminous.

"I'm good, just perhaps too much to drink today." She laughed and shook her head a little, her eyes closing for good measure as she held onto him with one hand and onto her drink with the other.

"Drinking on the job? I might have to let you go." He laughed and turned, offering his arm to her.

"Or just strike me out, as it were." She smiled, sliding her arm into his and shifting her drink to the hand closest to him so that she could lock her mask back into place.

His mouth moved in a smirk as his own mask moved into place, his eyes even more intriguing when accentuated with the black of the mask. The strength in his hands as he steadied her had ceased to surprise her, but caused that yearning to be something more than mere acquaintances or business associates to rise again from the pit of her chest.

"How was your afternoon? Enjoy your time at the salon?" He stopped near a large, ornate fireplace; the flames were low and only barely warmed the room, as the southern California cold was mild compared to what she was used to in New York.

She placed her drink on the mantle and turned to stand before him, moving toward him to keep their conversation intimate. "It was relaxing and incredible. Why are you pampering me? I feel like I'm in the calm before the storm."

He reached out and touched her shoulder, his eyes moving in the direction of his fingers as they carefully trailed down the curve of her arm. She shivered and wrapped her arm around herself, her eyes never leaving his handsome face, but simply waiting for him to bring his attention back to her inquisitive mind.

"I know that I've been secretive with you up until now, and honestly, I'm ready to start opening up a little," he said, retracting his hand and sliding it into the pocket of his perfectly fitted tux. "I want to start challenging you, to see if you're capable of being more than my assistant or my accountant."

She picked up her glass and took a quick sip of the icy-cold beverage, trying to make sense of what he was saying. Each time he spoke, soft shimmers of light seemed to move in the air around his mouth. It was charming, and yet it alarmed her to the core. It had to be the green dragon drink. Something was making her feel as if she were having mild hallucinations.

"What are you saying, exactly?" she murmured, sipping at her drink and watching his mouth more intently than she should.

"I want a partner, Ellie." He touched her arms again, bending a little before her and trying to catch her eye. Her staring hadn't gone unnoticed, obviously, and while she most likely appeared to be a lovesick school girl, the truth of the matter was that she wanted to see the shimmers again, simply to validate or discard their existence.

His words caught up to her a moment later and she gasped softly, her drink shaking precariously close to her dress. She moved back and the liquid splashed onto the floor; it was no more than a few drops, but enough to get her attention. "I'm sorry. This is all a lot to take in, and I had a drink today at the salon that I swear is making me see things."

He smiled and reached for her drink, taking it from her and setting it on the mantle again. "Did you hear what I said about our working arrangement? Are you at all interested in seeing if something could work out between us?"

She started to answer but was interrupted by a tall, thin blonde that put most centerfold models to shame. "Am I interrupting something? Sounds like David might be trying to commit to something more than financial wealth."

The woman laughed, and David smiled, shaking his head before looking toward Ellie. "This is Veronica Mills. She's an agent for many of the movie stars that you see on TV." He turned to Veronica. "This is Ellie, my accountant, who I was just talking to about partner consideration."

Ellie smiled politely and shook the woman's hand. The smell of her perfume was divine, but far too strong for Ellie's tastes. She watched Veronica's mouth as subtly as she could, noticing nothing out of the ordinary.

"Well, that's a relief. I thought you were asking for her hand in marriage." She turned to Ellie and laughed loudly, her perfect, blood-red lips curving up into a smile that could make angels fall. "What an incredible travesty it will be the day that David Kelley decides to settle down. We'd all lose our darkest fantasy, right?"

Ellie wasn't sure what to say, so she murmured, "Right."

David laughed beside her and reached for Ellie's forearm as he moved them away from Veronica. "Don't be silly, my old friend. I'm no one's fantasy. Just an honest guy trying to make an honest living. We'll catch up with you later. Looks like they're calling for us to take our seats for dinner."

Veronica waved them off and moved to the next handsome man in the room, Ellie's eyes following the bombshell. "Wow. She was incredibly beautiful."

David looked down at her as they walked to the dining hall. "Veronica? She's okay, if you like that type of woman, I suppose. She's very influential and knows more people than I do, which is saying a lot."

"And what type do you like?" Ellie asked, gaining confidence as they reached the long, decorative table before her. David pulled out her chair and stood behind her as she sat, his hands on the edges of the table on either side of her as he leaned in to speak into her ear.

"What type of what do I like?" he asked, and the air moved in waves, soft, blue, silky.

She turned to look up at him, reaching to pull his mask down and wishing she had the nerve to kiss him while he was being seductive. "What type of woman do you like?"

"Women like you." He left it there and stood up, doing what, she wasn't sure, but it didn't matter. There was more to this trip than clearing up her suspicions or joining him as a partner in the firm. He had something going on

inside of him that seemed to mirror what she had racing
around her own mind—curiosity at the 'what if?'

Chapter **Eight**

The sound of a fork hitting glass caused everyone to stop what they were doing and focus toward Ellie, her eyes glassed over as she was lost in thought. The sound of David's voice booming out from behind her caused her to stiffen, her shoulders locking in place as she sat up straight and tried to give off a professional appearance. There must have been eighty people at the tables around them.

"I wanted to thank you all for coming tonight. It's always a pleasure to see so many familiar faces in one room. I know you traveled from far and wide to celebrate my birthday with me. When I told Jean and Gen that I'd be happy to attend this event, I assumed it would be a small gathering with all of us in jeans and a t-shirt." David laughed and Ellie shifted in her chair to turn to look back at him, her head tilted up to see him better.

"Do you even own jeans, David Kelley?" a loud familiar voice yelled out from another table, followed by soft laughter that filled the room. David's smile widened and Ellie joined him; the brilliance of his demeanor and the beauty surrounding him was intoxicating.

"Yes, I do, but you people will never see them." He reached out his hand, and a member of the waitstaff placed a glass of champagne in it. Ellie was a bit surprised at how quickly people responded to his non-verbal call. "A toast, please."

"Now wait … aren't we supposed to make the toast?" An elderly gentleman stood up at the end of the table, lifting his own glass in the air. Ellie turned in her chair to watch him as his eyes filled with care for the man of the hour. "To the man who stepped up to take care of an old man when his kids had better things to do. You're like a son to me, David."

Another man stood up from across the table, lifting his glass toward David. "To the one who helped me claim what was rightfully mine and get my home back."

Ellie sat in shock, her eyes filling with tears as people from around the room lifted their glasses to the man behind her. In that moment she didn't care much at all how he made his money. At worst, he was a modern-day Robin Hood in her eyes. The moment changed things a bit for her, so for tonight, she decided that questions and concerns could be damned.

The room finally quieted and David's voice rang out, warm and clear, strong and focused. "Thank you all for being here. I am no hero, but I am proud to call each of you friend. And for my own toast: to the woman who's kept me financially sound for the last two years. Please, meet my assistant and, hopefully, a future partner at Kelley Enterprises, Miss Ellie Miller."

Everyone lifted a glass, and Ellie reached for hers, raising it as well and then taking a long drink of it as everyone sat down and began to chatter with those closest to them. She sat in shock, both at David's recognition of her and, even more so, at the fact that today was his birthday. Having worked for him for two years, she should've been aware of this fact, but she seemed to be the only one in the room caught off guard by the fact that this was a birthday celebration.

She looked to her right as David moved in to sit down next to her, pulling his napkin into his lap and turning toward her. "I was serious about what I said."

She took another drink of her champagne. "Which part of what you said? There's been a lot said tonight that could leave a simple girl's head spinning."

He laughed, and she could swear that the air clouded with particles of faint glitter. "Good thing you're not a simple girl, Elle."

"I'm not," she said, smiling and moving back to allow the waitstaff to place a salad in front of her. The older man to her left leaned over and extended his hand toward her.

"I'm Jonathan Kepener, and from what I hear, no, you're not." He shook her hand as she worked to put two and two together. A smile rushed across her face as she gave a sound of appreciation.

"Oh, Mr. Kepener. I was working on your financials before leaving New York. It's so nice to put a face with a name, finally." She shook his hand a little harder and then pulled back, smiling shyly.

He laughed, and David's laugh soon joined his. She leaned back as David spoke across her. "She was working hard on your stuff, Johnny. We'll be by for dinner with you and Melinda on Sunday night to go over everything, right?"

Mr. Kepener nodded and reached to pick up his fork. "Yes. Melinda is more interested in meeting this fine young woman than in seeing you again, David. I'd say that's a feat in and of itself, hmm?"

Ellie followed the older man's lead, picking up her fork and asking a quick question before taking a small bite. Her stomach reminded her that lunch had been nothing more than a cup of coffee and a few cookies that the hotel had provided. "Why is that?"

"David has been my financial advisor for the last twenty years, and his father was my advisor before him, for as long as I can remember. Never in in all those years has a woman ever accompanied him to our home."

"Well, I'm the one who does a lot of the work on your books, so I can see why that would be different now." She turned to David. "Did you do the accounting before hiring me?"

He nodded and turned away from her as the woman on the other side of him started to ask questions about the 'lovely young lady' with him. Ellie rolled her eyes at how ridiculous this was. He was easily the most attractive man in a room of three hundred people, and yet no one had seen him with a woman before? She hadn't either, if she were being honest, but they were always in a professional environment during work hours. Seeing him with a female companion who wasn't a client during business hours would be weird. *Seeing him with another woman at all would be more than weird. Downright depressing.*

"He doesn't do any accounting that I know of." The old man picked up his roll and began to butter it as he continued to talk. "David works on my various businesses' investments. Some of the businesses that I manage from a people perspective actually belong to him."

"Wait … you manage some of David's businesses, and yet he's your financial advisor?"

He laughed and nodded. "Sounds convoluted, I know. I guess it is to some degree, but he's like a son to me, so I help him out, and he keeps me afloat with his business savvy."

She couldn't help but dig a little more. David was busy trying to answer the questions being posed by the woman next to him and didn't seem to be focused on her at all. "What businesses do you manage for him, Mr. Kepener?"

"Please, do call me Jonathan and warm an old man's heart?" He smiled, and the twinkle in his eye made Ellie think that a young man's soul lived in the body of the elderly gentleman beside her.

"Sure, Jonathan. What businesses do you oversee that belong to David?"

"There are several, but my favorite is La Champarian's. It's a lovely salon that takes only the finest of clients. Beautiful décor, great business plan and just fantastic employees." He smiled and sat back, placing his hands in his lap after quickly wiping his mouth. "That was delicious."

"Wait … you own La Champarian's or David does," she asked, only to gather her answer from her boss.

"I own it, and Johnny manages it. Well, Melinda really looks after the place." He leaned over a little, smiling at Jonathan, his arm brushing against Ellie's. She shivered and tried not to focus on how close he was to her. The smell of his aftershave mixed with the simple smell of his skin caused her to groan softly. He looked over at her with questions in his gaze.

"Sorry. I didn't eat much today, and the salad simply stoked the blazing inferno of my metabolism." She shrugged, still trying to piece together what it meant that David owned the hair salon. Didn't the girl that did her pedicure say that the owner was some magic genie guy?

She didn't say magic genie. That's ridiculous. All of this is ridiculous.

"Well, dinner is being served." He moved back as a plate was placed in front of him. Ellie leaned over, breathing in softly as she inspected his dish. Small pieces of beef, fish and chicken decorated the black glass in a pattern that looked more like art than food. She sat back, a bit of glee filling her as she received her own dinner. Letting her thoughts die in the face of the feast before her, she focused on eating and left the rest of the conversation unfulfilled.

Dinner was heavenly, and Ellie was almost concerned with fitting in her already tightly tailored dress, but once they moved from the table and resumed a standing position, she felt much better. She took David's arm as they moved through the hordes of people, most wanting to know more about her and to thank him for all he'd done for them. She couldn't help but anticipate getting him alone so that she could push him a bit on why he'd turned into a superhero over the course of his life, or rather how he'd done it.

"Let's go get some air, hmm?" He pointed to a balcony off one of the small alcoves as they moved through the wide expanse of the hallway. She nodded, more than happy to take a breather and remove her mask for a little while. A small ache had commenced in her right forearm from having to hold the small stick in place all night.

A tall male of Hispanic or Spanish descent stepped in front of David, a smile on his face that didn't exactly seem genuine to Ellie. He extended his hand toward her and smiled. "I am Victor Romales. It is nice to meet the mysterious and alluring Ellie at last."

She laughed at the slight drama in his introduction, but played along, placing her hand in his and curtsying a little. "It is nice to meet you, Mr. Romales. I do hate to disappoint, but I'm sure mysterious and alluring are more fitting for another female here tonight."

"Victor. Always a pleasure. I appreciate you coming tonight. I know you must have traveled from far to be here, so thank you." David took the attention of the dark-haired man, and Ellie was almost glad to have his focus off of her.

"I wouldn't miss this for anything. To see you grow another year older, and yet you look as youthful as the day we met, David." His tone darkened ever so slightly, but Ellie picked up on it quickly. She moved back just a little to allow the men their conversation, turning to David and letting him know that she'd meet him outside when he was free.

He simply nodded toward her as she moved away, Ellie sensing something not exactly pure between the two men. She stopped at the door of the balcony and turned to grab one more glimpse of them together before moving outside. A soft shimmer of light moved from David's lips as he spoke. His facial features contorted just slightly, but it was enough for her to know she never wanted him angry with her. The perfect curve of his brow deepened, and he leaned in further toward Victor. Ellie took a step back, her heel catching on the door and causing her to reach out and grab the frame to steady herself.

It wasn't the light coming from David that bothered her, but the dark, pulsating smoke that outlined Victor's figure. If Ellie had been a believer in all things paranormal, she would've sworn she was witnessing a fight between the forces of good and evil. Yet, David didn't seem the angel in disguise. It had to be the drink. She turned and yelped as she plowed into someone who had stepped up behind her.

"Oh, I am so sorry. I should've been watching where I was headed." She offered up the apology as the boisterous redhead from the coffee shop stumbled back a little, but caught herself without too much effort.

"It happens to us all. I'm just glad I didn't flop over the edge of the balcony." She laughed loudly, moving to stand in front of the balcony and peering over the side. "I mean, can you imagine? How horribly embarrassing. To die from tripping. Ridiculous. Ridiculous, I tell you. Almost as bad as getting eaten by a shark."

Ellie pressed her fingers to her lips as she laughed loudly. "Embarrassing? I can't imagine dying being embarrassing, and yet I can't help but laugh. You are too funny, Ms. Barker."

The woman turned to look at Ellie over her shoulder. "You remember my name, child? We only met this afternoon."

Ellie nodded, moving up to stand next to her. The landscape below them was incredibly well cared for, with white lights decorating almost every square inch of the grounds. "Of course I do. I'm a businesswoman first and foremost." She always made a point to remember names when she was introduced. Besides, Sandra Barker was hard to forget.

Sandra nodded. "Yes, I see that. Tell me what else you are."

Ellie looked over at her, inspecting her in a way that was more curious than critical. The woman was beautiful in her own right, a bit large for a woman, but she carried it well, and her hair and makeup were pristinely done. Not knowing what to say, Ellie simply let the question sit between them for a few moments while she contemplated what she was, outside of being a professional.

"I'm a book lover and a runner. I suppose I'm a foodie, and I enjoy coffee and tea." She looked over to see if her answers had sufficed to receive a look that her mother had been giving her since she was a little girl.

"Those are things that you like, Ellie. I didn't ask you to tell me what you like, I asked who you are." She smiled in a way that made Ellie feel invited, welcomed. Earlier, in the coffee shop, the woman had effectively left her feeling like a simple secretary, like a wart on the side of a great and powerful man, but now, here … something was different.

"You're right."

"Of course I am, child. I'm a Seer." She left it at that and turned back to look deep into the night.

"What is a Seer, exactly? Forgive my ignorance."

"First tell me who you are, and then I'll explain what it is that I am." When she spoke, the air moved again, shimmering at first and then dying down quickly. Ellie leaned over and looked at her more closely, only to jolt at the sound of her laugh.

"I'm sorry. I swear, I keep seeing something floating in the air around you." She moved back and sighed softly, looking down at her hands and trying to coax herself into not feeling crazy. She knew for a fact that her head was playing tricks on her thanks to the liquor from earlier.

"Is it a fly? Get it next time, will ya?" She laughed and pressed her shoulder against Ellie's. "Answer my questions before David comes out here and interrupts us."

Ellie looked over her shoulder to see him moving their way. "How did you—?"

"Quickly. Who are you, Ellie?"

Ellie swallowed hard and looked back at the woman. "I don't know. I'm just a girl. I'm an accountant, but I want to be someone important. I'm just me, I guess."

Sandra pulled a card from her small purse and placed it into Ellie's hand. "Here's my card. Come and see me, and we'll talk further." She turned to leave as David approached.

"Wait … you didn't tell me what a Seer is." She took a step toward the lively woman.

The redhead laughed loudly and shook her head. "And you didn't answer my question yet either. Soon …"

David's hand on her arm caused her to turn toward him. A look of confusion appeared on his face. "Everything okay, Ellie?"

She nodded and smiled. "Yes. It's wonderful. Dinner was great, and it's been so fun to get dressed up for the day, but I have to know why you wanted me here."

He removed his hand from her arm and leaned against the balcony, his free hand working to undo the two buttons that held his jacket into place. She reached out to help him without thinking, heat rushing to her neck and face as she finished assisting and looked up at him, a bit of heat lining his gaze.

His voice was emotionless, but his eyes told her a different story altogether. To be the object of his attention was suffocating, powerful, dark. "You have been more important than you realize over the last two years, and I wanted you to experience a few things with me. One, I want you to know me a little better, and two, I want you to understand the business so that you can make the right decision as to whether or not you're ready to take another step in your career with me."

"How can you talk about us being partners when you barely know me? We've been crossing paths for two years, but have never really gotten to know each other." She felt her shoulders drop as the exasperation in her voice echoed in her ears.

"I hired you after much research into the perfect assistant and accountant for my business. Your resume speaks volumes, and the last two years have been a trial period, during which you've proven yourself independent, intelligent and capable of doing what it is that I do." He stood up straight and turned to look over the balcony, moving to lean on his forearms as the wind picked up and jostled his short, dark hair.

Ellie reached up and touched the side of her neck, her skin feverish and the cool night air doing little to offer her comfort. "I'm glad you trust me, then. I wanted to do well in my job, and it sounds like I have."

"And so much more, Ellie."

She looked over at him and tilted her head. "I don't know what that means, but I have a list of questions for you, so I'll just add it to them."

He turned to look at her and smiled. "How about this? Tomorrow night we'll go to dinner and talk. I have reservations for us at a great little restaurant downtown that only allows a few patrons in at a time. The place is quaint and inviting. You bring your questions, and I'll answer the ones that I feel comfortable answering."

She laughed and agreed with him. "I like the idea of dinner, just the two of us, so I can actually start working through the confusion that's still sitting in layers over my thoughts. But you evading all questions up to this point gives me no confidence that tomorrow night will be any different."

"Yes, well, some things are better discovered than delivered." He turned again and let out a soft breath, the air around his lips wavering with silky light. She boldly reached out and moved her fingers through the essence; the warmth of what remained coated her fingers. She brought them back toward her face and inspected them as David snorted softly next to her.

"What are you doing? I seriously suspect you did liquor up before the event tonight." He stood up and offered his arm, a playful grin on his lips. "It's getting late. Let's get out of here and head back to the hotel."

She dropped her hand and inspected him for a minute, her eyes moving across the thin line of his upper lip to the thick, full curve of his bottom one. It wasn't long before she was less worried about the essence in the air and more concerned with how it might feel to press her lips to his. She swallowed her desire and took his arm, nodding and moving toward the door, not trusting herself to say anything of value at this point.

Chapter **Nine**

Lights of every color bathed the car in a rainbow of sorts, as Ellie's mind slowly walked through the events of the evening. So many odd characters had stepped up to thank David for being important in their lives. He was multi-layered, of that she was sure. How that sat with her, she wasn't yet willing to probe. He wanted her to step up and be a partner in his firm, but one thing was for damned sure, she wasn't giving him an answer without specific details as to what would be expected of her and what it was that he did to make so much money.

She nibbled at her lip as they sat in silence next to each other. She glanced at David to find him staring intently out the window, his eyes almost glossy, looking lost in thought. It almost seemed a travesty to break the peaceful moment, and yet she had far too much on her mind to remain silent for much longer.

"Tonight was fun. Interesting." She turned a little, a smile playing on her mouth.

He looked over at her, his eyes moving a little in the dark across her face. She let the smile drop and just held his stare, hoping that he might find in her something he was looking for, someone he could trust and share his secrets with.

"It was interesting, to say the least. I never expected so many people to show up." His shoulders pressed back as he groaned a little. "I'm glad it's over. The old goat that invited me said that it would be a small affair. I realized when we ran into Sandra and she mentioned that the event had turned into a masked gala that I was in trouble."

Ellie laughed softly, crossing her legs and brushing her skirt down with her fingers. "I think it's endearing that you have so many people that you've helped. Like a modern day Robin Hood."

It was his turn to laugh. "I'm nothing like Robin Hood. Tights are not at all my style."

She smiled and shook her head. "I mean that you help those in need."

He shrugged, "It's simply part of who I am. I keep things in balance in the lives of those around me. Simple really."

"And what about Victor Romales? How have you helped him?" She knew she shouldn't push the subject after witnessing the high emotions that had sparked to life when Victor had shown up earlier in the night, but she couldn't help herself.

"Victor was once like a brother to me, but he became a bit obsessive with his, shall we say, calling in life, and I had to step in and reel him back. He's not been a big fan since."

"What do you mean, his calling in life?"

"I'll explain soon. He and I are cut from the same cloth, but he's much more passionate about what he does. I would quickly take the exit if given the opportunity." David turned to look back out the window. "Let's talk more over a drink at the hotel."

Without much to give in the way of a rebuttal, Ellie leaned back and reached for her phone. There were several text messages from her brother, going on and on about David's scar, which she'd noticed before, but it had faded in the background once she'd known him for a while. She had another one from Krista, complaining about her latest dating adventure that had turned south. Ellie laughed softly as she read through the tragedy that was Krista's dating life. She was glad that she'd pulled her name from a few dating sites after one or two mishaps, but Ellie still wished for a little more excitement in her life.

"What's funny, Elle?" David turned to look at her and she laughed softly again.

"My best friend has the worst time dating. I swear she has the worst luck of anyone I know. I was just laughing at her latest mishap." She continued to read her phone, realizing that her boss didn't necessarily want to have a conversation, but perhaps felt the need to be cordial and ask about the small noises of humor coming from her side of the car.

"And are you dating someone?"

That stopped her reverie. She slipped the phone back in her purse and looked over at him. The dark suit he'd worn that evening was still perfectly pressed and lined his physique beautifully. She swallowed before answering, hoping that her voice was more steady than she felt.

"No. I've dated a bit in the past, but I guess I just haven't found the right guy." She looked toward the front of the car as the driver announced their arrival.

"Shame," David murmured before slipping from the car.

Shame? Shame like I should have someone, or like you wish I were dating, or shame like shame?

"What do you mean?" she asked as he opened her door. She slid out and stood before him as he blocked her exit. "Why it is a shame that I'm not dating anyone?"

He leaned in as if he were going to kiss her, and her blood froze in her veins. His lips touched her ear as he whispered, "Because you're exquisite."

He moved back, having just leaned in to close the door. His hand wrapped around her upper arm and tugged a little, moving Ellie past him as the door slammed. Stunned and not too sure what to say at the intimacy of being so close to him, she walked into the hotel and exhaled a soft sigh of relief.

He moved beside her after tipping the bellman. "Do you want to change and meet me in the lobby for drinks or do you want to just go like this?"

"I'm fine staying in this if you're okay with it."

"I live in a suit, so I'm perfectly comfortable." He offered his arm and she took it, and then they walked to the small restaurant and bar. The hostess gave them a quiet table in the back of the restaurant, small white candles lighting up the space before them.

After ordering them both a drink, David leaned forward, placing his forearms on the table. Ellie watched him like a predator might watch its prey, wanting to know what his every move might mean, needing to understand what he did and who he was, desperate to uncover his thoughts about her.

"Ask, Ellie. I know you have questions, so now is your chance. After tonight, no more digging, only the fact finding you can do yourself from the places I take you and the things I introduce you to."

She nodded, trying to grasp what he meant, but deciding that an open invitation to ask questions was more enticing than trying to figure out what tomorrow might hold. "And you'll answer anything I ask you?"

His eyebrow rose sharply. "I'll answer what I'll answer. That's more than a fair deal."

"Fine. How did you get into my house the other night?" Her shoulders stiffened as she put on the best business façade she had.

"There was a key above the door in the back. I got the key and put it in the lock and walked into the house to wait for you."

"Didn't you think you'd scare me to death? I could've shot you or something."

He smiled wryly. "My turn."

"Your turn? What do you mean, your turn?"

"I get to ask a question for every one you ask," he said very matter-of-factly before reaching up and taking their drinks from the server.

"That doesn't seem fair," she spouted, her temper rising.

"And why not? I have questions about you too, Elle."

She tried to think of a reason that it didn't seem fair that she should have to waste time answering stupid questions about herself when she was anything but interesting. This wasn't a game of 'you tell me this and I'll tell you that.' This was her trying to decide if her boss was safe enough to … to … *to what?*

To let into my life. My bed. My heart.

She sighed loudly, much like the unruly teenager she once was. He laughed in response. "Fine. Ask me a question, and I'll answer it to the best of my ability."

He took a sip of his drink, reaching down to undo the one button holding his jacket together at his waist. "Good. Why do you have a key in such a readily available place for burglars?"

"Where else am I supposed to put it?"

"Anywhere but under the mat or on top of the doorframe. Put it in the little blue and gold potted plant that hangs by the back door. Move it when we get back home. Yes?"

She was more taken aback by his detailed description of the potted plant at her house than his demands. "Fine, yes. I'll move it."

She leaned back in her chair, thinking through all of the questions she wanted to ask him and landing on an easy one for now. "What is it, exactly, that you do to make the kind of money you make?"

"I'm a Balance Keeper. I ensure that people have balance in their lives. If they don't, I do whatever is necessary to restore it."

His response made no sense at all. "So, you're a shrink, a bouncer or an advisor?"

"All of the above on some occasions. That was two questions. My turn."

"That wasn't two. That was a follow-up question." She smirked, knowing that she was caught and hating him temporarily for it. "Damn. Fine."

His fingers played along the length of his thigh as he seemed to ponder his next question. She had no idea where this might go, but was willing to play along, simply to have the right to ask another one of her own questions. "Why were you and your brother following me a few nights ago?"

"You really did see us out there?"

"That's a question. I want a response to mine first." He tilted his head knowingly.

"I wanted to know what you did for a living."

"You're my accountant and you don't know what I do to make the money that I make?" he asked in a tone that wasn't condescending, but not necessarily uplifting either.

"I know you're in a service business and that you have over ten thousand clients, from what I can tell."

"Right. I'm a Balance Keeper. Everyone needs balance in their lives, Ellie. You need a little too, don't you?" He leaned forward again, his eyes deep green like the belly of the sea.

Her body tightened, shoulders stiffening again as she found it hard to breathe. "That's one too many questions, Mr. Kelley. My turn."

"Well played. I like it." He rolled his shoulders, reaching up to undo his tie. Ellie couldn't help but follow his movement, the strong muscles of his neck and chest flexing as he tugged at the thin material.

"I don't know what a Balance Keeper is, but will you show me over the next few days while we're here?" She turned her gaze toward her drink, the icy liquor giving her a break from the vision before her.

"Absolutely, but you'll have to keep your eyes open. I'll point it out here and there, but your perception of what I do will be as important as what I actually do. You'll have to make the choice of whether or not to join me when the weekend's over."

His hand moved across the table and slipped over the top of hers, the roughness of his palm causing her hormones to spike painfully. *When was the last time I felt a man's hands on me? Oh yeah … it's been forever.*

"Do I scare you, Ellie?" He spoke softly, but the deep timbre of his voice wrapped around her as she tried to figure out the foreign emotions that beat against her. Fear? Worry? Terror? No. Lust? Desire? Longing? Yes.

She looked up at him, her lips touching the small glass she held in her hand before taking one long drink to finish it up. "No. I wish you did, to be honest. I'm intrigued, and I want to know more about you than I've wanted to know about any other individual, but I'm not so sure that's a healthy place to be."

He took one last gulp of his drink, finishing it, before standing. "I'm not so sure it is either, but I plan on letting you in further than anyone else in my long history has been invited, so you should feel both blessed and cursed, I suppose. Come, let's go to bed."

She stood up, her knees shaky at the idea of going to bed with him. Did he simply mean that it was time for them to turn in—in their respective rooms—and go to sleep? Or was he asking for something else? She shivered at the thought and moved around the table as he smiled down at her.

"Cold?"

"Something like that," she mumbled and walked through the lobby with him. The hotel staff was working hard to remove the fall decorations and get the Christmas décor in place. Ten to twelve young looking employees moved about, stringing lights and garland while the sounds of Christmas played through the speakers at the front of the hotel. She smiled and enjoyed the scene before her, her own thoughts a little too nefarious for reviewing with present company.

They slipped into the elevator and she turned to face him. "I'm not even close to being done asking questions, David. That was the tip of the iceberg."

He turned to face her and took a step forward, closing the space between them until there was only enough room for a small sliver of light to pass through. "I understand completely." His finger touched the bottom of her chin, and the slight pressure caused her head to tilt up, her eyes locking onto his.

"There won't be a need for direct questions after tonight because I plan on giving you a firsthand view of who I am. I told you at the party that I want you to think about partnering with me, and I wasn't being trite. I need a partner, and fate has determined that person to be you, so like it or not, you and I will be working closely together for a long time. Ask whatever plagues you most, Elle. If I feel like you need to know something, you won't need to ask, because I'll already have shown it to you."

Breathless and tingling from head to toe, she tried to stay cognizant in the moment and keep up with the words that slipped from his lips. The golden essence she'd seen earlier was there, but muted and softer, more appealing somehow. She let her gaze move from his mouth to his intense stare and back down again, the sharp slope of his cheekbones so regal and defined.

"You said I was exquisite tonight, that I was beautiful. Did you mean it?"

He leaned down and stopped just before her, the soft breath of his mouth on her lips. She wanted to close her eyes to prepare for what she prayed would be a kiss, but couldn't force herself to miss seeing him up close. Looking into the depth of his eyes was like getting lost in a moment forever, never wanting to surface and yet needing to breathe so badly. His fingers brushed across her hip and outer thigh, and she sighed like a lovesick puppy.

"Painfully so," he whispered before brushing his lips across hers, his tongue lapping once at her mouth before he moved back and walked out of the elevator, the door having opened on his floor. She slouched against the wall of the moving contraption, her eyes wide, her breathing sporadic.

"Hells bells," she murmured before slipping out of the elevator on her own floor and walking on legs made of jelly to her room. Not only was she going to work at finding out exactly who David Kelley was. She needed a serious game plan to make him hers.

Chapter **Ten**

"You did what? Holy hell, Ellie. What were you thinking?" Jacob's voice growled through the phone as Ellie lay on the big fluffy bed in her hotel room.

"I didn't do it. He did." She'd tried explaining the kiss to her overprotective brother, but as per usual, it wasn't going well.

"Why would he kiss you?"

She sat up and huffed. "Why wouldn't he kiss me?"

"I mean that this is a business trip and he's a professional. Well, he's supposed to be. Obviously he's just a pervert."

"Jacob, you're being ridiculous. It was a quick peck on the lips, like an affectionate moment between friends," she explained, wishing she'd have never mentioned it to him now that she had.

"You're not friends. Sell this bullshit to someone else. I want you to come home."

"Well, I'm not coming home. I'm a grown ass woman and the sooner you realize that, the better."

He started up again, but she cut him off, warning that the conversation would be over if he didn't let it go. With a little more warning, he finally piped down about it. They sat in silence for a few moments before he sighed loudly and changed the subject.

"Did you check for the scar above his eyebrow like I told you? I mean, you were definitely close enough to get a peek at it." He snorted.

"I've noticed it before, but I don't see how it's so very important. Oh, I did go to a very odd birthday party for him yesterday." She sat up on the bed. The large white robe wrapped around her was worth more than all the clothes in her closet added together, she was sure.

"Why was it odd? Did he turn a year younger instead of older? He's a vampire. I knew it!"

"Not funny. No, it was just that there were so many people there, and they all seemed to know him, but not really know him." She brushed a small piece of fuzz off the pocket of her robe.

"Kinda like you."

"Yes, but each of them shared something he'd done in their lives to make things better."

"Like Mother Theresa?"

"Something like that, but he called himself a Balance Keeper. Not sure what that means, but I'm going to find out. He owns like half the town, from what I can tell, and it's like he can read my mind and see the future."

"How many drinks have you had, lush?"

"Only a few, but something is going on here, and I'm seriously jonesing to figure it out." She stood up and walked to the balcony and moved the curtains aside, giving her a perfect view of the nightlife that occurred just below her.

"Just be careful, okay? I already didn't like this, and the kiss thing honestly makes it worse. Just don't let him take advantage of you, and don't tell me you don't like him, because I know you do."

"You're my twin. You should've known that I liked him when I made you do that stakeout with me." She laughed, and Jacob joined in too before giving her a few more words of warning.

They spoke about their mom and then about her cat, Marx, before hanging up. She sat the phone down near the TV and walked back to the balcony, opening the door and stepping out into the mild winter wind. The sounds of horns and laughter bubbled up from the street far below, but quickly became swept away in the whisper of the wind. She closed her eyes and tugged the sides of her robe closer, enjoying the warmth of the soft cotton and the cold of the elements all in the same moment.

The kiss had been hot, and it filled her imagination with so many scenarios, none of them ending in her behaving in a manner that her mother would be proud of. She sighed and placed her hands on the railing, leaning over a little and thinking back to her conversation with Sandra Barker.

Who was Sandra in David's life? They didn't seem quite friends, and yet she was full of joy to be at the party tonight. She'd slipped away as David had approached, obviously wanting to talk with Ellie, but not with the birthday boy. Why?

And Victor. Cut from the same cloth as David, and yet the two of them seemed to be a dual-action bomb waiting to go off in each other's faces. Victor was smooth and elegant, like Old World money, and David was dominant and aggressive. The two should be at each other's throats, but Ellie suspected there was a lot more to that story than one might ever imagine.

"Any way you dissect it, there's still way more that I don't know than what I do." She turned and walked back into the hotel room, carefully closing the door behind her and locking it. No need to invite Dracula to bed with her tonight, though if he resembled David at all, that might not be a bad idea at all.

Ellie moved toward her suitcase, and kneeled in front of it, digging in her bag for her old journal. Then she grabbed a pen and slipped into bed. She fluffed up the pillows behind her and settled down to scribe something about the day so that she'd remember it in a week, a month or a year from now. One of the most traumatizing things in her life was waiting for the early onset of dementia, just as she had suffered through with her mother. At only fifty-nine years old, her mother barely remembered anything from her past. There were days when she couldn't seem to figure out who Ellie and Jacob were. Ellie was terrified at the idea of having something so horrible happen to her. So, if she was damned with that fate, she'd have enough journal entries to make sure she'd never completely forget all the great memories that lay in her past.

She spent thirty minutes writing about the oddity of the day and the weird encounters at the party that night. A few more minutes on the conversation with David and the kiss, and she smiled, closed the journal and laid it on her stomach. The day had been long, but good. Of course, the weird situation with the flowers from the night before hadn't made it onto the list of questions for David that night, nor had the green dragon drink, or the fact that her name was his password four years ago when they didn't even know each other.

"Damn … you wasted the night asking about him breaking into the house and whether or not he thinks you're pretty. So many questions and you asked the stupid ones."

She growled and picked up the diary, needing something to read before she spent half the night berating herself on how silly and childish she could be at times.

Skimming through various entries from several years back, she saw nothing that grabbed her attention until her entry on January 5th from her junior year in college. The small design in the middle of the page accentuated the words 'gold dust.' Ellie sat up and pulled the large journal closer to her face, starting at the top and skimming through the page. It had been a normal day of class, and only when she'd agreed to meet her TA for coffee had things gotten interesting. She remembered that day like it was yesterday, and yet, like every romance she'd tried to start in the last four years, nothing had panned out.

"No surprises there," she muttered as she continued to read through the day. The journal said that when she'd finally finished all her homework and cleaned up the small apartment that she and Jacob were sharing at the time, she walked languidly down to the small coffee shop on campus. She'd picked up a double espresso with one sugar and then sat happily on the patio, waiting for Wes, her TA, to arrive. He was cute and quite sweet, or so her journal read (the lies before the truth was discovered). A couple of older men sat to her right, deep in conversation. One of them kept looking her way, and the reason the scene made it into the bowels of her journal was because he held an uncanny likeness to her brother. It was as if she were looking into the face of her brother in twenty years.

She sat back on the bed and tried to remember the day, her mind not giving way to the exercise. A soft sigh left her lips as she bent over to read what else had happened. The entry said she'd waited for Wes and glanced at the men a few times, realizing after a while that, when they spoke to one another, golden dust seemed to puff from their lips. She thought herself crazy that day and made sure to document that in the journal as well. After today's events, she wasn't so sure.

"There was golden dust in the air around David's mouth tonight." Was it a new drug? A trick of the eye? What the hell would cause something like that? At least knowing that she'd seen it before David gave her some small affirmation that she had, in fact, seen it again with him today. "At least I'm not going crazy. Or maybe that's just a future entry I've yet to write."

Questions popped up, begging her attention, but between the high emotions, the drinks and the long day, she was beyond tired. After tucking her journal back into her bag, she turned off the lights and let the nightlife outside her window sprinkle the room with brilliant colors. Tucking herself into the warmth of her sheets, it wasn't but a few minutes before she let the darkness take her under.

"It's going to take one more time, Ellie." The voice belonged to a man she didn't know. Gold dust swirled around her as she knelt in the middle of a large, grassy field. Her hands lay before her, splayed out on the large chest of another man, his head turned from her, and his chest still.

"I don't know if I can," she whispered as heavy emotion pressed down on her. A sadness stronger than she could ever remember feeling before slammed into her, and she groaned at the weight of it, her head falling forward, long chestnut hair falling over the body below her.

"You can, baby. You must. We cannot do this without him. Find the light within you and force it to burn brighter. Do it, Ellie. Do it now."

She groaned again, her fingers pressing into the flesh and muscle of the man in front of her as the one beside her continued to offer her encouragement. She moved her hands up the chest, her long fingers digging into the solid structure of the man's chin before pulling softly to get his face to turn toward her. She tilted her head to give attention to her coach beside her and gasped softly as the older looking version of her brother smiled down at her.

"Who are you?" she asked, the dense realization of who he could be playing along the edges of her memory.

"I am the weakest part of you. Do what we came to do."

"But I don't know how to do it. I'm scared. What if I fail him? What if I fail you?" She felt the hot burn of tears and swallowed hard, not wanting to look down and yet unable to face the father figure beside her much longer. "Where were you all those years?"

"There isn't time for this now, Ellie. Save him."

She turned and moved toward the handsome man below her, his skin cold and face laced with the signs of death. A cry left her lips as she pressed her mouth to his and breathed with force, an explosion of gold essence filling his mouth and bringing color back to his skin. She moved back, wiping her mouth as the man coughed a few times; his breath was ragged, but he was breathing.

"Is he going to be okay?" she asked, turning to ask her father more questions, questions she already knew the answer to. He was nowhere to be found, but she didn't have time to ponder that. The man below her reached out and grabbed her arms, pulling her down to lie across his chest. His large hand cradled the back of her head, and the other pressed to the small of her back as he sucked in fresh air.

"Thank you," he whispered. The feel of his strong arms wrapping around her caused her to relax and melt against him. So many worries and needs lay hidden in the deepest valleys of humanity, but in that moment, gratitude for a life renewed was all she needed. She wrapped her arms around him too and pressed her lips to the smooth skin of his chest. He would be better than alright. He would be strong and renewed, and together they would change everything. She just needed to know one thing.

"Did you know my father?" she whispered and turned to look into the eyes of the man she'd loved for eternity. "Did he know you?"

Ellie woke with a scream lodged in her throat, the cold air of the room attacking her half-dressed body and giving her extreme chills. Sweat lined her PJs and forehead, her heart racing and fear rushing around in circles outside her consciousness. She sat up on the edge of the bed and pressed the palms of her hands to her temples as she tried to slow her breathing down a little. A dream had pushed her past the point of comfort, and now her body was trying to determine if the extreme emotion was real or simply an illusion.

"Just a dream, just a dream, just a dream," she murmured to herself before standing up and stretching her arms to the ceiling. The clock read two a.m. and, for its efforts, received a huge groan from her. She moved to the small table in the room and turned the light on, standing there for a minute until her eyes adjusted. The beautiful flowers David had sent over the day before sat perfectly straight and ready for attention. She reached over and caressed one of the rosebuds before picking up the small message card and reading it.

"What are you doing in my dreams?" She shook the card in the air as she threw her accusations around the room. "I need sleep and will see you in the morning, and yet you just can't stay away. You just have to jack up my sleeping hours, too, with your sexy hotness."

She dropped the card and knelt before the small mini-bar, pulling out a cold bottle of water and drinking half of it before needing to stop for a breath. It took too much effort to get up, so sitting down on the floor seemed the better idea. Ellie stretched her legs out in front of her and took her time drinking the chilled water and trying to remember the details of the dream. There had been too many weird events in the last few days, and something nagged at her senses—a warning.

Maybe understanding David wasn't the best idea. People had skeletons in their closets for a reason, and thanks to him, not only was she pining after her boss like a fifteen-year-old girl with a crush, but she was having horrible dreams about a man that seemed to be her father. But surely not. She'd never met the man, nor had Jacob. He'd disappeared out of their lives before they were born, and their mother never said a thing about him.

The day she'd written about seeing a man that looked similar to Jacob, she'd asked her mom a few questions about their dad, but she was rewarded with the silent treatment and the same old story about him leaving a few months before their mom gave birth to them. Something about that day at the coffee shop and the remarkable likeness to her brother gave her pause and made her question her mother's story. She needed to know more about that area of her life, but first things first—David.

If she was savvy enough to figure out who he was and what he was up to, then she should be a private detective. After the David mystery was put to bed, literally, then it was on to finding out all she could about her father. Whether Jacob would be down with helping or not was up in the air. He was more sensitive about the subject of their dad, but she couldn't blame him for that. No boy should grow up without a father, and yet Jacob had done just that. Ellie finished her water and then climbed to her feet and made her way back to bed, leaving the light on.

"Too damn scary in the dark," she grumbled and reached for her diary, owning up to herself that it was just going to be *one of those nights.*

Chapter **Eleven**

Morning light filtered through the open window, the frigid cold air causing Ellie to snuggle down deeper in her covers. She must've left the air conditioner on all night long. She turned just enough to see the clock on her bedside table and groaned out loud. She hadn't really made plans to meet David at a certain time, but it would be nice to spend the day following him around in hopes of getting a little closer to her goal of discovering his secrets. She pulled the covers back and shivered, rushing around the room to get dressed quickly, pulling on black tights and a soft, cotton sweater.

Making sure to close the curtain before heading out, she texted her illustrious boss to see where he was and if they could meet up. She received a text back a few minutes later, informing her that he was already in the bistro downstairs waiting on her to wake up. She grumbled about early birds as she slipped into the elevator. Her hair was spun into a tight bun, and a thin red and black scarf was wrapped around her neck. She walked quickly toward the bistro, her jacket slung across her arm, the only sound of her approach being the heel of her black boots on the freshly mopped tile floors.

The hotel staff had truly outdone itself in terms of holiday decorations. Lights and garland hung from the walls and balconies, and the Christmas tree that sat near the front door was easily the biggest one she'd ever seen. A sense of joy swept over her, and her face wore a large smile as she wondered what her brother and mother were up to. She rarely decorated her small house, but they always made time to decorate her mother's house. Jacob had lived with Ellie for years, only moving out to help their mother as she continued to go downhill in the last few years.

Sadness touched her features as she approached the table where David sat, his eyes already on her. She slipped into the seat across from him and let herself take him in, the smell of his soap and cologne filling her senses and causing her to breathe in deep, hoping for a little more. He wore a black sweater over a white oxford shirt and black corduroy slacks. Most men couldn't pull it off, but he did it beautifully.

"Why the frown?" His voice was more gravelly than usually, like he'd just woken up or was getting sick.

"Just thinking about my mother. I need to make sure to get over to her place and decorate it for the holidays." She shrugged, hoping that he'd move past the topic, but of course he didn't.

"Why does that make you sad? Is something wrong with her?" He picked up his coffee cup, coughed into his fist and turned his attention back to Ellie.

"She has one of the worst cases of dementia her doctor has seen, at least for her age." She motioned for the waiter and ordered a cup of coffee with a little bit of space for creamer.

"Wow, that must be incredibly hard on you and Jacob." David sat his cup down and leaned forward, Ellie feeling the weight of his stare.

"Yeah, but we're used to it. She's had it since I was a little girl. It's only in the last few years that it's gotten so incredibly bad." She paused and thought about his last statement. "How did you know Jacob's name?"

He smiled, obviously enjoying her discomfort. "You've told me a little about your brother. He's your accomplice when you sneak around to find out information on your poor, unassuming boss."

She smirked and shook her head, grateful for the warm cup of coffee placed before her. "That is true; however, my boss is anything but poor. Man's filthy rich, and you know the craziest part?" She leaned forward and looked around the restaurant as if she were divulging a great secret.

David leaned in too, his face softening, which made him look like a boy, melting her heart more than she cared to admit. "What?" he whispered, as if filled with awe and wonder.

"I have no idea what he actually does." She sat back with a very knowing look on her face. "I believe he's either a pimp, a drug dealer, a bookie or perhaps the devil himself."

David laughed as he sat back, picking up his cup again. "I think the first three options are just ridiculous. Those people don't make the kind of money that we do. The last option … well, I've heard he kisses like the devil."

She felt her cheeks heat as the look on his face moved from innocent to pure sin. She had to answer him, but a quip was far from her thoughts. Her mind replayed the scene in the elevator the night before, and she could do nothing but agree with him. "That he does."

"Sorry to interrupt, folks, but could I get you anything but coffee this morning?" The waiter looked down at them as Ellie cleared her throat.

"Yes. I'd like a bacon and mushroom omelet, potatoes and toast." She slid the menu toward the younger man and turned to look at David, who waved the boy off. "Not eating?"

"I had a few pieces of toast earlier while I read the paper." He patted the paper beside him. "I have to meet with a few clients today. I'd like you to come with me."

She nodded, working to make her coffee perfect as she felt excitement wrap itself around her. "I'd love to. I want to know everything before making a decision on partnership, and if I understood you correctly last night, my decision is expected at the end of this weekend."

"That's right. I think you'll enjoy today. The people I work with are really good people. It's been a long time since I've had to play on the wrong side of the fence. Doing good is much more fun than doing ill."

"Doing ill?" She felt her brow crease, thinking more about this idea of him being a 'Balance Keeper.'

"Don't worry too much about that right now. We're in a good place to do some positive work in the world. I'm looking forward to having you help me as soon as you learn the ropes."

She heard a slight buzz, and he reached into his pocket, pulled out his phone and then stood. "I need to take this. I'll be back shortly."

Ellie sat back and placed her hands in her lap, her mind rushing about in an effort to try and put a few more pieces of the puzzle together. Doing good for society was something she most certainly wanted to be a part of, but doing ill? What did that even mean?

The waiter approached and offered her a top-off on her coffee, but she kindly declined, letting him fill up David's cup as she turned to look for her boss. He was out of sight but far from out of mind. Whatever he was up to was going to be put on display later that day, and as much as she looked forward to it, the one thing that captured her thoughts more than any other was the remembrance of his kiss the night before. He was so proper and professional, and yet his affections the night before had shown her a completely different side of him. It was a side she wanted to explore.

"All in good time," she whispered to herself, moving back a little to allow the server to place her breakfast before her. The smell was heavenly and her stomach growled softly in appreciation.

"Someone's hungry," David said, his voice moving past her as he took his seat.

Ellie nodded before digging in, not caring too much about being dainty and proper. She and David hadn't been around each other much over the last two years, so they hadn't gotten to know each other on a personal basis. Though she was fit and well proportioned, she rarely skipped a meal, and pretending to eat less than she usually did or in a manner that wasn't her style was out. She groaned at the rich taste of the cheese and bacon as it hit her senses, a smile brushing across her lips as her eyes met his.

"I love that you love to eat," he said, sitting back and crossing his arms across his thick chest. "Most women refuse to eat in front of men, or at least they don't eat the way they'd like to. Did you know that?"

She finished her bite, took a quick drink of the water sitting in front of her and nodded. "I actually was just thinking that I didn't care what you thought of my eating habits. I love to eat, and if someone has a problem with that, well so be it."

"Someone being me?" He laughed.

"Well, yes." She picked up her fork and began cutting her omelet up, her cheeks burning at the thought of him being important to her and of her divulging that fact. "However, you're just my boss at present."

He smiled. "Yes, let's wait until we've formed a partnership for you to become focused on what I think about things."

She almost responded by asking what type of partnership he might be referring to, but decided to let the conversation die. She focused on eating her breakfast and noticed David checking his watch a few times. "Do we need get going?"

"In thirty minutes or so. No huge rush. We'll be meeting with Mr. Pierre this morning. He's a client of mine." David finished speaking and emptied his coffee cup, placing his hand over the top of it as the waiter appeared. "No, I'm good. Just charge the check to my room, please."

"No problem, Mr. Kelley. You enjoy your day." The younger man quickly cleared the table and left with a smile on his face.

Ellie sat back, full and happy. "Jean Pierre? The one that owns the flower shop?"

"Yes. Have you been to his shop before?" David asked as they stood. He motioned for Ellie to follow him to the hotel lobby.

"Yes. I went over there yesterday because you sent me flowers." She moved in front of him and stiffened a little when his hand pressed against the small of her back.

David's brow creased as he looked down at her. "Were you going to send me flowers in return? That seems a little odd, but I guess if it's something you're accustomed to …"

Ellie stepped into the lobby and stopped, turning to meet his gaze. "No. I wanted to know when you wrote the card that was with the flowers."

"You went all the way over there to ask when I wrote the card? Why not just simply ask me? I would've told you that I wrote the card when I ordered the flowers." David's eyebrow raised, as if questioning her sanity.

She growled softly toward him, crossing her arms across her chest defensively. "The card was written weeks ago and yet it answered a question I asked you *in my head* last night, David. How do you explain that?"

He laughed, and the sound wrapped around her, golden flakes of ether floating about. "Now we're getting somewhere, Elle. Grab your coat and whatever else you need from your room and meet me in the car. I'll answer you on the way to Jean Pierre's shop."

Ellie stood there for a few minutes as David took his phone out of his pocket and began talking to whoever had interrupted them. The long strides he took to the door gave her reassurance that she definitely knew one thing about him—he was dominant and in charge. She rolled her eyes at the thought of liking that side of him more than she should. A quick trip to her room, and she was ready to encounter whatever the day had to throw her way.

She walked out into the cool mid-morning air and jogged toward the open car door, the driver smiling at her as she approached. "Good morning, Miss Miller. How are you today?"

"Very well, thank you for asking." She slipped in beside David, who was wrapping up his call. "Everything okay?"

He looked over at her and nodded, his face a mask of indifference. "Yes, just trying to decide who to contact to help me with a new client that's causing trouble in New York."

"Causing trouble?" she asked. The heater was working overtime in the confines of the car, and it wouldn't be long before she'd have to tug off her coat. She imagined that the cool morning air felt cold to native Californians, but it was nothing compared to the New York weather she was used to.

"Yes. I think getting Victor involved would be the best move for us." He turned to look out the window, the conversation dying between them as the driver pulled out into the busyness of the morning. Ellie wanted to bring up the flower mystery again, but knew by the denseness of the silence that David was deep in thought about a mystery of his own. She'd hit him up later over the message and, more so, the timing of him writing it.

His response had caught her off guard back in the hotel, and as disturbing as it was, the gold dust hadn't. She'd almost begun to wonder why she'd only seen it the night before, allowing herself to believe that perhaps she'd made it all up. The very fact that, within the pages of her journal, there existed another man that had the same ability, gave her pause. *Maybe it was him?*

Her thoughts dissolved as they stopped in front of the small flower shop, the driver turning to wish them well. She slipped from the car and moved to walk beside David, who walked past the front door and moved into a small alley between the flower shop and a donut shop. She followed, staying right behind him as they moved in silence. A few raps on a rusty old door, and Pierre opened the door wide, a look of sadness on his features.

"Hello, my old friend. Come in." He moved back as David moved in and motioned for Ellie to join him.

"Jean, you met Ellie last night at my party. She's my new partner, so please don't mind her being in attendance with me." He moved toward a small office, walking in as he spoke over his shoulder.

Ellie moved in beside him and took a seat at a small table with three chairs. *Almost like he knew I was coming, too. Odd.*

"I trust you completely, David. If you think Ellie should be here, then so be it." The older French man looked to Ellie with a warmth in his gaze that reminded her of her grandfather who'd passed a few years back. "Ellie, it's nice to see you again."

She extended her hand and shook his. "It's nice to see you as well, Mr. Pierre."

David motioned for Jean to have a seat. "Tell me what you're dealing with, Jean."

Jean sat down, leaning back in his chair as if his bones were ready to give out. "You humor me, David. You know exactly what I'm dealing with. You knew before I called you that this was to be. Why should I speak my tragedy out loud?"

David nodded, his face softening a little. "I know, but Ellie has yet to figure out that she knows as well. Please, for her benefit, explain the problem so that we can go to work fixing it."

Ellie sat up straight in her chair, her senses on high alert. How would she know what the issue was? David most likely knew because Mr. Pierre had been a client for a long time, and it was obvious that the two were close. The comment threw her off a little, but she worked hard not to show her discomfort.

Jean breathed out and nodded, his voice shaky when he began to speak. "It's my daughter, Genevieve." His eyes moved from David to Ellie, and she felt as though the air had been sucked from the room. "She has been running with the wrong crowd lately, and last night when she left, I begged her not to go, but she just insisted that she's an adult and can take care of herself."

Ellie nodded and reached out to touch the older man's hand, which shook slightly on the table. His eyes filled with tears, and Ellie absently rubbed her chest just above where her heart sat. The pain filling the room had started to suffocate her, and damned if her own eyes didn't fill with tears, her empathy on high alert.

"She's yet to come home today, and I just know that something bad has happened to her." He looked to David as a few tears trickled down his face. "She's dead, isn't she, old friend?"

David spoke and the air turned gold around him. "No, Jean, she's not. I have very little time to get her back before she is, though."

"Where is the balance sitting right now, David?" the man asked, and Ellie tilted her head to the side as she moved her hand from his.

"There is too much bad." David stood up and motioned for Ellie to as well.

"Oh, thank God," Jean whispered and laid his head on his forearms as he began to weep.

Chapter **Twelve**

Ellie walked quickly behind David, her mind trying to discern what had just happened. The idea that Jean's daughter was missing and in danger was horrifying, but the rest of the meeting was what scared her the most. She slipped back into the car and listened as David barked out directions to the driver, letting the man know that they were in a hurry. He sat back and looked at Ellie, reaching over to take her hand.

"Okay, download what you're thinking and let's talk about it. I need you to have full disclosure if you're to make a conscious effort to move into this lifestyle." He turned and took her face in his hands, his own face a mask of indifference. "Everything we discuss is just between us. Do you understand me clearly, Elle?"

Ellie nodded as best she could, her heart beating a million miles a minute. He removed his hands from her and took her hand back into his. "Talk to me. I need to know what you're thinking in order to tell you the rest of the story."

She swallowed hard and started as best she could. "I'm heartbroken that Jean has lost his daughter, and yet somehow I think I knew that she wasn't dead. But maybe that was just me being hopeful."

"No, you knew."

"And then the part where he said that you already knew that she was missing and you said that I already knew it too … what the hell?"

"I'm a Balance Keeper and you are as well. You'll learn to listen to all of the moving pieces around you as I train you. I know what is happening in all places around me, and when I hone in on something specific, it's like looking through a microscope. He mentioned the girl, and I already felt her presence at the address I gave the driver. I'll teach you all of this as well." He squeezed her hand as if they were talking about her breaking a heel or stubbing a toe.

She pulled her hand from his and gaped at him. "Do you know how ridiculous you sound?"

He nodded. "Yes I do, but you'll learn that if you simply open your eyes to what is real and what is just smoke and mirrors that you too will start sounding ridiculous."

She smiled in spite of herself. "Why is it a good thing that there is bad in the world?"

"What?" He looked over at her. "It's never good when the balance shifts to the darkness."

"Exactly, so why is it a good thing that there is bad in the world?"

"Are you referring to Jean's admission to being happy about there being more bad than good in the world right now?"

"Yes." She turned her body to face him, her knees pressing into the side of his thigh. He let her hand go and laid his own on her knee, as if they'd been lovers for years. Her eyes moved to the connection as she felt her breathing become a bit shaky.

"Ellie, there always has to be balance between the darkness and the light." He stopped, as if he were contemplating how to continue. "As a keeper of that balance, if there is too much good in the world at the time a decision is to be made on my part, then I have no choice but to serve the darkness. The flipside of the coin is also true."

She sank into her seat a little, her mind finding recognition in his words. "You're saying that if the balance in the world was more on the side of good right now, you'd let the girl stay kidnapped?"

"I'm saying that I would not be able to interfere, thereby, allowing her to die." He looked away, his gaze filled with a foreign emotion that she'd yet to see there before.

A soft gasp left her lips, and she pulled her legs away from his touch. "How could you do that to her? And honestly, how do you know the balance of the world? You sound ridiculous."

He placed his hands in his lap and mumbled as the car pulled to a stop, "They aren't my rules, I simply answer to the rules' maker."

He opened the door and walked quickly toward a large warehouse, the roof sunken in and the walls dilapidated to the point of almost falling in. Ellie got out of the car quickly and caught up to him, fear rushing through her. "What do you think you're doing? We could get ourselves killed out here."

He looked over at her and smiled, a bit of darkness touching his features. "Never. Just watch and learn, Ellie. This is what I'm asking you to step into with me. How deep you're willing to go is a question I told you is yours alone to answer."

She stopped as he continued to move forward, the heaviness of his words trying hard to break through the fire spreading through her from the look in his eyes. She grumbled a few choice curse words to herself and caught back up with him. Why did he have to be so damned good looking?

So incredibly hot that I'm willing to walk into my death to feel this alive again?

The sound of male voices filled the hallway before them, and David looked back over his shoulder to remind her to be quiet, as if that was at all necessary. She placed her hands on her hips and gave him a look her mother would be proud of, as he ignored her and moved forward. The hall was dark and smelled heavily of must and death. The door at the end of the hall spilled light into the narrow hallway, and Ellie could feel the tension of whatever was occurring on the other side way before reaching it. David looked over his shoulder, his hand on the handle.

"Watch what I do and simply stay back." He nodded at her and she returned the gesture.

They walked through the door, and it took Ellie a few minutes to focus on the scene before her. The beautiful young French girl who'd helped her with her flower question the day before stood in the middle of the room, her shirt half torn from her body and her face bloody and bruised. Her hands were tied above her head by a chord of some sort, and three guys who looked to be in their early twenties stood next to her, arguing over who was going to have the pleasure of killing her. They looked toward David and Ellie as they walked into the room.

"Hey! Who the hell let you in here? This is private property, you dumbass." One of the guys, a tall, muscular man, moved toward David, his hand reaching for something tucked in the back of his pants.

Ellie yelped and moved back a few steps until she hit the wall behind her. Gen looked up, and Ellie felt her heart drop. Suddenly, Ellie could read her thoughts. The girl knew she was going to die and was so filled with sorrow at leaving her father alone to deal with life. Jean had lost his wife a few years earlier to a robbery in the store, and Gen was all he had left. The tie around Gen's mouth suffocated her screams as she started trying to communicate with Ellie.

Ellie felt a calm rush over her, almost like someone pouring refreshing water over the top of her head. She stood from her cowering position and started toward the girl, her mind completely on helping Gen get free. She forgot all about David and the three men, and time seemed to slow for a moment. Laser focus became hers, and she narrowed her eyes, her senses picking up on the screams from Gen's obstructed mouth.

"Get out of here, now. Go please. Tell my papa that I'm sorry. Get out of here, now." The girl repeated herself over and over as Ellie picked up her walk to a run, her heart beating faster as the world seemed to shift back into place. She reached up and tugged on the ropes, groaning a little and getting nowhere. Quickly, pulling the small gag from the girl's mouth, Ellie started to talk to her.

"It's going to be okay. David and I will get you out of here." She realized then that she'd left David with the three large men. She mumbled his name and turned to survey the scene before her, fear racing along her nerves that something might have happened to him.

To her amazement, two of the men lay on the floor, and the third one stood in front of David like a small boy, her boss leaning over him with his hands on the guy's shoulders. Ellie felt her jaw drop, and for a moment, she almost wished she would've witnessed whatever had occurred. David looked up at her, his eyes filled with warmth, and he motioned her over. She started to go, but the sound of Gen's cry gave her pause.

"Don't leave me," she whimpered. "Please, please don't leave me here."

Ellie looked around and found a chair and a knife, grabbing both and climbing up to cut the rope that held Gen in place. "We came to get you, not leave you." She wrapped an arm around the girl's exposed shoulders and walked toward David.

"Ellie, set the girl down in the chair and come here. I want you to see my gift." He spoke in a voice that was almost hypnotic, and Ellie found herself nodding and moving Gen to the nearby chair she'd just used to free her.

"Sit here and I'll be right back. We'll get you out of here and home safe to your father." She hugged the girl tightly before moving toward David.

The third guy involved in Gen's attack stood before David like a statue, his eyes glossy and his mouth opened as if he were completely lost to reality. Ellie moved beside him, her eyes searching out evidence of what had occurred before looking at David. "What's wrong with him?"

David placed his hands on the younger man's shoulders and leaned down, seeming to be in direct eye contact with him. Ellie watched closely as gold dust filled the air between David and the thug, David exhaling it, and the guy breathing it in. Shock crawled across Ellie's senses, and she found herself backing up, only to be caught in David's stare as he turned his head to focus on her. The rims of his eyes were as gold as the dust that moved through his lips. "Watch, Ellie."

She nodded and planted her feet on the ground, her hand reaching out and touching a nearby table to keep her balance. She knew in that very moment that everything was about to change. She could kid herself that things had been odd and a bit unusual the last few weeks and that there was a lot of explaining to do, but after this moment … reality would shift.

David turned back to the young man. "Kade, do you hear me?"

The guy nodded, drool running down the side of his mouth and dripping from his chin. Ellie focused on the stream of saliva and found herself overwhelmed by the fact that his saliva had evidence of the gold flakes.

"Good. Here's what we're going to do." David breathed in deeply and exhaled, sending another large puff of shimmering gold rushing into the air. Kade breathed in deeply, and Ellie covered her mouth with her hand. "You're going to call the police and let them know that you and your friends here kidnapped a young woman and were intending to kill her, but you let her go."

He nodded again and Ellie felt her knees go weak. She leaned on the arm that held her up and closed her eyes for only a moment. What had David done? Hypnotized the guy? Then what was the dust?

David continued. "When they ask why you're calling to tell them this, you simply tell them that the guilt of it all is eating you alive. Tell them that you knocked your friends out and called to turn the three of you in."

The guy nodded again and Ellie stood up as Gen approached, her eyes wide with wonder as she watched David. He moved toward the kid, pressing his lips to the younger man's forehead, and Ellie stood in shock as the young man crumpled to the ground. David turned toward Ellie and Gen, his eyes still ablaze in an unnatural way as he reached out and took Gen in his hands, his fingers gripping her shoulders. He breathed out and she gulped the essence in.

"Gen, none of this ever happened. You broke up with Kade last week and your father is happier for it. You spent last night sorting through various types of roses and, not listening to your old man, decided to try and go down into the cellar even though the light's broken. You fell down the stairs and busted up your beautiful face, and your father patched you up and told you to take the day off. Do you understand me?"

Ellie watched as the girl's features went slack and her head bobbed with understanding as David spoke. He leaned in and kissed the girl's head, catching her as she crumpled toward the ground. He maneuvered her into his arms and walked toward the door they'd entered only minutes ago and stopped briefly by the door as Ellie realized he needed her to open it.

"Oh," she mumbled and rushed forward, her legs on fire with the desire to give out and her mind close to breaking. She opened the door and walked close to him as they made their way down the hall.

He whispered in a voice that sounded laced with laryngitis as they left the warehouse and entered the sunny mid-day, "I need rest. Take her to Jean and tell him the story I told her. I'll meet you back at the hotel in time for dinner."

The driver opened the back door of the car, and David leaned in, placing the sleeping Gen in his spot before turning to Ellie and touching the side of her face. "You were brilliant today."

She stood there, unable to speak, as he smiled at her and turned to walk toward the road behind them. Ellie turned to look at the girl before finding her voice, but when she turned back to question her boss, he was nowhere to be found. *What the hell?*

"Miss Miller. Are you ready to go?" The driver stood in front of his open door, his hand on the door Ellie stood near.

"Yes. I suppose David is going to walk back to the hotel." She shrugged as the driver laughed.

"I took Mr. Kelley back to the hotel while you were in the building. He said he would meet you for dinner. Everything alright?" The driver tilted his head, a look of worry crossing his face.

Ellie nodded and turned to walk to her side of the car. "Yep. I need to drop Gen off with Mr. Pierre at his flower shop."

"No problem at all."

"Thank you, Ellie. I cannot thank you and David enough, honestly." Mr. Pierre's hands squeezed Ellie's shoulders as he stood before her, his face looking worn and thin.

"It was really all David's doing, Mr. Pierre."

"Please, call me Jean." He smiled and moved his hands from her.

"I'm just glad she's okay and that we got there in time." Ellie smiled and walked toward the back door of the flower shop. "You have the story down that I told you, right?"

He nodded. "Absolutely. Tell David that I love him like a son and that I still would have no matter the result of today's events."

Ellie stopped in the doorway and crossed her arms over her chest. "I will. Can I ask you one thing, Jean?"

"Anything. I owe you both everything I have. I lost Gen's mother, Lucinda, a few years back in a robbery, and it changed everything for us. My little girl is all I have." A sad smile played on his face.

Ellie felt overwhelmed that she already knew the intimate details of Jean's life, and simply because fate had assumed she needed to understand a muted Gen earlier. She squeezed her arms tighter, as if hugging herself in comfort against the unexplainable weirdness that circled her.

"How long have you known David?" she asked, trying to steady her voice and not succeeding at it very well.

"Since I was a little boy and got caught in a rushing river on the east side of town. My father called upon David, and he answered, saving my life, much like he saved my Gen's life today. I am forever indebted to him for his service to the creator of life." Jean smiled and Ellie let her hands drop to her side.

"Are you telling me that the David that rescued Gen today is the same one that rescued you, as in not a younger version of him or perhaps his father who looks much like him, but the same thirty-something year old David Kelley that I work for?" Ellie couldn't believe the ridiculous words that were coming out of her mouth, but then again, with all that had just occurred, foreign and unbelievable were finding new definitions.

"You asked for one question, child, and I answered it. Who David is and how long he's traversed this earth is a question that only he can answer." Jean pulled her into a warm hug and thanked her again before shutting the door and waving through the window.

Ellie waved back and walked numbly back through the alley and into the street. She thanked the driver for opening the door and slipped into the silence of the back seat, her arms quickly wrapping around her again to offer what little comfort could be found. "What the hell is going on?"

Chapter **Thirteen**

Ellie leaned in close to the mirror in her hotel bathroom, her body covered only in a large white towel. It was the middle of the day, and yet nothing but a hot bath seemed appropriate to warm her up. Her eyes moved along the small indentations around her mouth, which her brother had always called smile lines. She needed to see if there was any remnant of the golden dust on her. Some part of her feared the idea of having something so powerful near her, around her—on her. She inspected herself, finally sticking her tongue out and ensuring that it, too, was simply pink.

"You're being ridiculous," she told her reflection firmly.

"Am I? What the hell was that stuff?"

She moved back, pulling her hair into a tight bun at the top of her head and sighed loudly. The stuff David breathed out was obviously some sort of hypnosis drug. When someone breathed it in they turned into a mind-numbed zombie that would be willing to turn themselves in to the cops.

"But what about falling asleep when he kisses your forehead?"

The remembrance of the soft kiss she'd received from him in the elevator the night before had her wanting to do anything but fall asleep. She laughed and stepped into the steamy water, sinking to her knees and moaning softly at the warmth that surrounded her. A hot bath always did the trick, no matter what ailed her—this made it better.

The soft, yet insistent ding of her phone caused her to sigh angrily. "What it is? Why does everyone seem to know when I get into the tub? Damn phone never goes off unless I'm in the tub."

She decided to ignore it, moving from her knees to her butt and enjoying the next round of goose bumps the water afforded her, only to hear the phone again. What if it was her mother? What if something had happened to Jacob, or worse yet, what if David hadn't made it back to the hotel, but was passed out on the side of the road? What if he was dead?

"Oh, for God's sake." She stood up and reached for her towel, wrapping it around her and stomping into the bedroom to get the phone. She grabbed it off the table and walked back into the bathroom, dropping the towel and getting back into the water, her enjoyment lost to worry.

One text message kept causing the disruption as if it were screaming for attention. *Odd.* It was from Sandra Barker and simply said to come and have tea with her at two if Ellie was free. There was a reminder that the address of her shop was on the card she'd given Ellie the day before. Ellie texted back that she'd be there and then sent off a quick note to David that she'd meet him for dinner at seven if he was free. She wanted to add something about making sure he was okay or that she was just checking in on him as well, because she felt like she was being a bit too formal. Still, perhaps the kiss from the night before was just a quick moment of lust, thanks to the multiple drinks they'd had that night.

"But what about him touching my knee today?" She placed her phone on the side of the tub and sank back into the hot water, her thoughts slipping from the oddity of the day into the soft press of David's lips on hers. Hopefully this trip would end with all of her questions answered, a new partnership formed and maybe even a love story that was just in its inception.

She smiled and let the giggle that bubbled up in her chest dance across the air in front of her. It would have been a pleasant moment if the shimmer that normally belonged to David alone hadn't rippled from her soft exhale as well.

"Hello?" Ellie said as the soft jingle of a bell announced her arrival at Ms. Barker's store. She walked into the warmth the small space provided and called out again. "Ms. Barker? It's Ellie."

Something rustled in the back of the store, and Ellie assumed that it was Sandra making her way to the front. She stopped to inspect a small counter that held over a hundred items for purchase. The story was like a runaway flea market of sorts, items scattered everywhere, some of them recognizable and some not at all. Several vials of green liquid shimmered, as if the substance were moving on its own in the confines of the small tube. Ellie picked one up and turned the vial to read its contents. "Green Dragon. Why does that sound … oh, hells bells. The drink I had at the hair salon."

She put the vial back down and walked to the door, sticking her head out. Sure enough, the street signs validated that she was at the corner of Broadway and Main. The chick that had painted her toenails told her that the magic of the green dragon drink was from this shop, but the owner was supposedly a man. She slipped back into the store and almost ran Sandra over, both of them yelping.

Ellie reached out to touch the other woman's shoulders. "I'm so sorry. We need to stop running over each other like this."

Sandra laughed and shook her head, her red curls wild and beautiful. "I think it's good to be startled now and again. Keeps us on our toes and aware of the life we've been given to guard." She turned and motioned for Ellie to follow her. "Come with me to the office so we can talk."

Ellie followed behind the large woman, her eyes still moving along the various items for sale and not finding much that she recognized. It was a specialty shop, alright. Ellie just wondered who the customers might be and how these odd trinkets sold at a rate that kept Sandra employed.

"Do you own this shop?" Ellie spoke to Sandra's back as they walked into a small, well-kept office.

Sandra turned and sat down in a large leather chair behind a small desk. "Oh, I don't own it. David does, actually. I just run it for him from time to time. We don't actually keep the doors open for anyone to come in like most stores do. It's special order only, so most of the things on the shelf have either been ordered or will be in the near future."

"Will be ordered? How do you know that? Just repeat customers that keep getting the same thing year after year?" Ellie sat down in a smaller chair and sank down into the worn black leather. The fact that David owned the shop didn't surprise her much, but with the greeting David and Sandra had shared the day before in the coffee shop, it didn't seem like they'd seen each other for quite some time. How can you be in business with someone and not see them? *David and I do that all the time, actually.*

"I told you last night. I'm a Seer." She smiled with a knowing look on her face and lifted an eyebrow at Ellie. "Do you have an answer for me from last night? I'm quite ready to spill my secrets, but I want to know yours first."

Ellie shifted a little bit in her seat. "I wish I knew a secret that I could share."

Sandra smiled and the room lightened a little. "Tell me what you did with David this morning."

Ellie coughed and felt her cheeks burn. "We helped a girl out of a bad situation."

"Did you help him, or did he do it all on his own?" Sandra asked, crossing her arms across her large bosom.

"He did most of the work, but I did cut the girl down. It was so weird, honestly. I swear I've been seeing things since drinking a green dragon drink." She paused and watched for movement in Sandra's features, but got none. "You have the *magic* found in the drink out in your shop."

"David's shop, but it's nothing more than an elixir to open the eyes of those that can already see the supernatural and choose to ignore it." She paused for a moment and then spoke again. "Why do you think David chose you to be his partner, Ellie? This question will help you determine who you are."

Ellie thought about it for a minute and wanted so badly to answer with things that made sense. She was organized and smart, confident and studious, but those weren't the answers the overbearing woman in front of her was looking for. "To be quite honest, I don't know."

"That's as good an answer as any. David will tell you the why when the time is right." She removed her arms from across her chest and leaned forward, placing her forearms on the desk between them. "You said the other night that you were just a girl and that you wanted to be someone special. I will tell you now that you are quite special, and over time you will get the chance to see that become evident."

Ellie began to fidget, her fingers brushing along the front of her skirt as her gaze focused on the movement. "I'm not sure what you mean, but I hope you're right."

"What happened today when you left David? I assume you saw something that gave you a bit of concern?"

Ellie's eyes moved up to fix on the older woman's. Something knowing swept across her warm and welcoming face. "What do you mean? I've been seeing things I shouldn't since I came on this trip with David. Things that, if I shared, might make me seem crazy."

"I have seen everything you've seen today and all that you will see tomorrow. I am a Seer and a Balance Keeper alongside David." She tilted her head, dark red curls bobbing as if dancing about. "I know what happened with Jean and Gen this morning, how David and you both saved the girl's life. I know you will be great one day and will slip into your role as comfortably as David and I have slipped into ours, but what I don't know is how you feel about what you saw in your bathroom today."

"The golden dust?" Ellie felt her heartbeat pick up as her palms began to dampen. Fear wanted to tug her into silence, and yet for the first time in the last few days, she felt like she had the opportunity to discuss everything with a straightforward individual who might help her work through some of this.

"Yes. David's gift is one of yours as well, you just don't know how to use it yet."

"I can do what David did with his golden dust?" Ellie reached up and touched her lip as it quivered. "I thought maybe I had just inhaled some of it. What is it exactly?"

"It's his gift. He is the keeper of good. When the world is out of balance, which it is at most points in time, David is able to use his inherent goodness to re-level things, so to speak." She paused and Ellie tried to think through the implications of doing good all of the time.

"But he mentioned that sometimes good cannot be done and ill must be the tool." Ellie sat up in her chair. "Was he saying that he has to do bad things or let bad things happen as well?"

"He doesn't actively do bad things, but the force under which we serve does tie our hands in all situations. David is only allowed to employ good if the world is out of balance, with the darkness winning ground."

"And who employs bad if the light is winning?" Ellie questioned, her voice sounding more mousey than she might like.

"That is a conversation for another day. Each member of our group will disclose themselves to you at the proper time. For now, David is to train you in the way of the light and I am to help both of you by opening the door to the future when the time is right."

Ellie nibbled on her lip as her phone buzzed in her purse. "You can see into the future? Like the gift of prophecy or something?"

"Nothing as biblical as that, but I can see into the future from now until the end of time. I can focus on a place and time and gather what will be and how our Balance Keepers must react. David and I are linked as one, seeing that we were created to work in tandem with one another."

Sandra nodded toward Ellie's purse as her phone buzzed again. "Do you need to get that?"

Ellie felt her eyes go wide at the unbelievable story she was being told, but was grateful for the break in insanity as she reached into her purse and pulled out her phone. It was her brother. She declined the call and texted him that she'd call in a few minutes, after her meeting. He texted back that it wasn't an emergency but that he had more information on David and wanted her to call ASAP.

"Sorry. Just my brother." Ellie sat back and slipped the phone back into her purse.

"Jacob. He's a great boy and will be a fantastic father to three kids one day." She smiled and tapped her fingers along the desk. "Now, back to what we were talking about. What questions do you have, child?"

"Ummm …" Ellie was caught up in the fact that Sandra knew her brother's name and seemed so sincere in the fact that she could read the future. Would Jacob get married and have three kids? She wanted to ask for more details but felt unsure about asking for information about a time yet to come. Did anyone truly want to know the future? If they knew, was it set in stone or was there a way to change it, even up to the last minute?

"It's a lot to take in, I understand." Sandra sighed softly and stood before saying, "I'm grabbing a Coke. Would you like something to drink?"

"A green dragon seems fitting right now." Ellie laughed and Sandra did too before walking out of the room. Ellie sunk back in her chair, her breathing loud and rapid, as if she'd run around the block a few times. Was all of this for real? None of it made sense, and yet she'd seen every bit of it with her own two eyes. She'd wanted to come on this trip and wanted to know everything about David and what exactly 'client services' entailed, seeing that his main stream of revenue left her at a dead end.

Sandra returned and placed a cold Coke before her, and though Ellie rarely drank soda from the can, she sat up and gulped down half of it before catching her breath. "I'm just a little overwhelmed by all of this. I think the main question I have right now is … why me?"

Sandra opened her Coke and nodded knowingly. "I understand that one. I think it's going to be David's place as your guardian to answer that, but your conversation with Jacob in a little while will open the door of understanding as well."

"My guardian?"

"Yes. It's rare to have a new Balance Keeper added to our group, but it has happened in the past. You are the second one, so there's still a lot to figure out. The creator requires you to have a guardian to partner with you and teach you about your specific gifts so that you can carry the weight of your position alongside the rest of us."

"You sound like a crime fighting team." Ellie laughed and took a quick, nervous sip of her soda.

Sandra scoffed. "Nothing of the sort. We rarely use violence. Our tools are much more powerful than anything you've seen."

"Unconventional as well," Ellie mumbled, thinking back to David kissing Gen and the young men on the forehead that morning. They were knocked out, with no fight left in them.

"Very much so. David's goodness, or the gold dust you keep referring to, brings people into a comatose state and suggests his will upon them, rendering them and their desires useless. He doesn't need to fight or bring a weapon, because the power of suggestion attacks the deepest parts of a person's persona and will do the trick every time."

"What about the kiss on their foreheads?" Ellie whispered, setting her Coke down as she felt a sense of wonder wrap around her, the air before her illuminating with dust. She swatted at it as if it were something evil, yelped and stood up, knocking her chair over.

Sandra stood as well and walked around the desk to touch Ellie's shoulders as she looked down at her. "It's nothing to be afraid of, Ellie. It's a lot to take in, but you have the power of positive suggestion too. David bends the darkness to the light, and you have that ability as well."

Ellie licked at her lips, tasting nothing but the sugary goodness from the Coke. "It is scary. To be introduced to a world you didn't know existed is one thing, but to be a part of it … something totally different."

"Agreed. I cannot fathom how hard it must be, but I do know that you have an excellent teacher in David. He will train you in utilizing good to fight back the darkness." She squeezed Ellie's shoulders and moved back a little, still holding on.

"I guess. Why are there two of us fighting for the side of light, or are there more?"

"There is only one, which is David. I'm not sure if he's going to transition into being the core of the group and become the holder of all gifts, or if that position is for you to hold." She shrugged and let go of Ellie, running her fingers through her hair.

"The core of the group? What does that mean?" Ellie picked up her chair and slumped down into it, her fingers brushing by her lips again as she studied the digits to see if there was a remnant of what had just occurred.

"There were five of us, but we lost a member a short while back. The fifth member was the Core, meaning that he had all four of our gifts and one of his own. With him gone, someone has to take his position or we can quickly become imbalanced ourselves. I'm not sure if David is moving into that position or if that is you."

Ellie felt herself grow defensive quickly. "Do I have a choice in any of this? You're talking like it's already a done deal."

"I can see the future, Ellie. You're in it, and it is a done deal. What I cannot see is the division of power between you and David. It's too blurry, for some reason." Sandra closed her eyes and touched her brow. "Either way, you agree to step into this because you realize that this great power must be guided by someone and used for the purposes for which it was created."

Ellie sat there for a few moments, trying to sort through everything Sandra had shared with her. She knew she'd stepped into a whole new world the minute she'd crossed the security booth at the airport. All of the small bits of information she'd gathered seemed to make sense now. David didn't have the ability to see into the future, but Sandra did. He must've asked her for help. But why?

"I will tell you this, child," Sandra started, her eyes opening and illuminating to become the brightest blue Ellie had ever seen. "All of the questions you have will be answered by the one that has claimed guardianship over you. He will protect you and guide you, but you have to be completely willing."

Ellie reached for her Coke before standing, the end of their time together drawing near. "I understand. I think part of what I need to do this afternoon is to really search myself and see that I'm ready to answer David when he asks if I'm willing."

Sandra stood and smiled. "I think we both know the answer to that, but appease yourself and search deep. There is so much more under the surface than what you can see, so do yourself a favor and trust your instincts over the facts you've collected."

Chapter **Fourteen**

"How was your afternoon?" David sat comfortably in his chair at dinner, his oxford shirt fitting him perfectly and tucked into his navy slacks. He looked ready for a round of cocktails and a game of golf. She found comfort in his presence and loved the way her stomach tightened every time he spoke. To say she was smitten would be an understatement.

"It was interesting." She eyed him over the rim of her cocktail, her thoughts jumping between their rescue mission that morning and the odd conversation with Sandra Barker. She knew the truth of what was before her, but couldn't understand how believing it didn't make her certifiably insane.

"Oh, yeah? Tell me about it then." He leaned in, the soft candlelight of the restaurant illuminating the perfect curves of his face—high cheekbones and perfectly straight nose, thick eyebrows and a gaze that set her heart on fire. The slight lift of his eyebrow was a nudge to talk, and yet she wanted nothing more than to sit and stare at the beauty before her.

She coughed into her hand and set her drink down so as not to spill it. "What happened this morning with Gen and Jean … I want time to think through it, and honestly, talking with Sandra this afternoon helped a lot. I'm still not sure what it all means, but I'm starting to see that there is more going on around us than we could ever imagine."

David smiled and placed his arms on the table in front of him. "I'm glad you went to talk with Sandra. We've been friends for a long time. She's a good woman, and we use her gift so often that I'm not sure how she's not completely worn out."

"She looked alive and well when I visited with her today." Ellie reached over and touched David's clasped hands, her gaze touching his. "I was worried about you today. You walked away from the warehouse this morning looking beaten. Why didn't you just come back with me?"

He moved one of his hands to cup it over hers. "I needed to gain my energy back and knew someone needed to speak with Jean and get Genevieve back home. Thank you for doing that. I feel much better now."

"Of course, but that doesn't make up for causing me to worry about you, David," she said with a soft growl and removed her hand.

"I understand, but you'll soon find out that when we're called into action, there's almost always two of us together. One using their gift and the other to clean up the mess. When we use our gift it drains us for a time, and rest is the only antidote." He shrugged as if it were nothing.

"Walking five miles back to the hotel is not what I would consider resting." She shook her head at him as the waiter approached with the dinner specials. Ellie ordered the fish, and David went with the steak and potatoes special.

"I can transport from place to place, Ellie. Every one of us can." He spoke softly, picking up his drink and taking a long sip.

Her jaw dropped a little. "You cannot."

"Yes, I can. I'll show you when the time is right." He sat the drink down. "I'm thinking a little at a time might help make things easier for you to swallow."

She simply stared at him, torn between thinking they were both crazy and knowing the reality of what had happened earlier that morning. She needed to change the subject. "So, Sandra tells me that you are a member of a five person group and that she's the Seer and sees into the future."

He nodded. "She is our Seer, yes. Right now, the group is only four members strong. We lost our fifth member a couple of years ago." Sadness touched his features briefly, but he covered it well by taking another drink.

"Were you close?" Ellie asked softly, unable to let it go.

"Yes, very. He was like a brother to me." David brushed his fingers along the table. "He was my best friend and has been since I first walked the earth. To see him perish is bittersweet."

"How so?"

"Well, I miss him terribly and don't have the comfort of his companionship or his guidance anymore, but to know that he's resting with the creator … blissful. I cannot imagine what it will be like when my time is up. I keep expecting to feel weary from all of this, but it's yet to happen."

"The creator, as in God?"

"Something like that, yes." David smiled and moved back a little, placing his napkin in his lap as the waiter approached with their salads. He waited for the man to move away from the table before continuing. "Tell me what you thought about what happened with us this morning."

"I think it was scary, adventuresome and beautiful. Saving someone's life? I never would've imagined in a million years being involved in something incredible like that." She picked up her fork and poured the small cup of ranch dressing all over her salad before mixing it and taking a quick bite.

"Do you have questions about how I did what I did?" he asked as he worked to get his salad mixed as well.

"I did before talking with Sandra, but I think I understand it better now." She took another bite and tried to work through all of the things she wanted to talk to him about, but there were almost too many of them. They jumbled up her thoughts and left her numb to wanting to know more.

"You'll spend some time with me over the next month, should you choose to partner with me, and then I want you to spend some time with Sandra as well."

"Why do I need to spend time with Sandra?" Ellie asked as she looked up from eating.

"Because we need to discern whether you are replacing me or replacing our lost member. I would assume your placement will be where he once was, but I need to be sure. If you work with Sandra and gain her ability during that time, then we'll know for sure."

"She said that he was the Core. She explained it a little, but to be quite honest I'm overwhelmed and not sure I can handle having your gift, much less all of his." She picked up her roll and began buttering it. "Why was I picked to do this, and who picked me?"

"The creator picked you for reasons that will be made obvious to you over time." He spoke very matter-of-factly, his eyes moving across her face and leaving her a bit breathless.

"You say that as if you know it."

"I do know it. Sandra has shown me a great many things about you and our future together, Ellie. At this time, we have to walk through all of the details and introduce you to our way of life. The responsibilities that have been placed on us and the agreement to remain secretive are going to be crucial."

She nodded, grateful that he was her guardian and the one that would teach and train her. *Is there a rule against falling hard for your guardian? If so … consider it broken.*

"What are you thinking?" David asked as he placed his napkin on his plate.

"That I'm glad you're my guardian. Not sure what that means either, but knowing that I'm in the hands of someone that represents the light and that I feel like I can trust gives me peace."

"I will show you all that I know, and that which I don't, we'll figure out together."

The server showed up and placed their meals before them, and they slid into casual business talk and shared small details about themselves with one another. Ellie enjoyed that the conversation had changed from things of a world she was just now discovering to one she'd known her whole life and felt quite comfortable with. Dessert was a treat beyond her imagination, the chocolate tower they shared being built for ten people (and yet, almost devoured by two).

David stood at the end of the meal and moved to help her up, a warm smile on his handsome face. "That was fun and delicious. Tomorrow I'm playing golf with Victor, so sleep in and enjoy yourself, and we'll get together in the afternoon to see if there's anything, work-wise, that we need to focus on."

She nodded and turned to walk out of the restaurant, her phone buzzing numerous times by the time they'd made it to the elevator. David slipped in and pushed the buttons for their floors as his own phone began to buzz. He checked it and answered quickly.

"What's up?" His voice was all business and rather intimidating. She could hear a masculine voice on the other end of the phone, but couldn't make out the words the caller was saying. "Yes, I understand. Have her go back and change it then."

"No, it is that easy. I cannot keep expending my resources when you have your own to give to the project." He paused again as the door opened to his floor. He reached over and touched Ellie's back, gave her a quick wink and then he was out the door, his voice gaining volume and intensity. "You'll do it because I said you'll do it—period."

The door shut and Ellie backed up, having found herself standing at the front of the elevator, completely captivated by the man she worked for and the conversation he was having. Who needed to put more into whatever was going on? Did he actually have business clients outside of being a Balance Keeper? How did Balance Keepers make money? It's not like good deeds and working for God would put someone in a place of financial freedom, would it?

"If working for God doesn't make you financially stable, then what would?" She laughed as she exited the elevator.

An older couple walked past her down the hall, and the man responded to her. "Nothing, young one."

The man laughed and Ellie did too, shaking her head and pulling out her hotel key before moving into the silence of her room. Her journal lay on her bed, as if beckoning for her attention.

"Soon," she mumbled and started to pull clothes from her body. Not getting another kiss from David in the elevator left her wanting one even more, and yet there was something that felt a bit forbidden about having a relationship with her boss. "And, let's add guardian and fellow Balance Keeper to the list," she mumbled to herself. "Balance Keepers. What a weird name for a group."

She shrugged and slipped into her PJs, grabbing her phone from her purse and plopping down on her bed. Dinner had left her full, fat and happy, but the coming conversation with her brother was sure to bring in a bit of homesickness. She rarely traveled, and being away from her mom and her brother around the holidays was putting a damper on her spirits every time she stopped to think about it.

The phone only rang once before Jacob picked it up. "Hey ... damn, I called like ten hours ago."

"It wasn't ten hours, and I told you I'd text or call you a little later," she said with a huff as she worked her way down into the covers.

"Yes, well, it's a good thing I didn't need blood. ASAP stands for as soon as possible, not as soon azzzzit pleases you."

She laughed, enjoying the comfort of her brother's voice. "That isn't a word."

"What izzzzn't a word?"

"Never mind. What did you need? Is Mom okay?"

"Yeah, she's fine, your cat is fine and your friend Krista is super fine. Did she tell you that we bumped into each other in the store the other day?" He whistled and Ellie rolled her eyes. "Hook us up, Sis. Like, for real."

"What did you need? I'll talk to Krista about you when I get home, but I'm sure she sees you like a little brother too."

"What? Why? We're twins. You're not my older sister by more than a few seconds."

"Slow your hormone roll and answer my question."

"Fine. Hook us up when you get back." He paused and then continued, the soft purring of Ellie's cat coming through the phone and making her more homesick. "I started to look through some old photos today, and you'll never guess what I found."

"Missing me that much, are you?"

He laughed. "What are you, Yoda? No I'm not missing … wait, yes, I am missing you, but the photos weren't of us or you, but of Dad."

She felt her chest tighten. Their dad was a subject they'd let die among them many years ago. He'd been around to make them, but didn't stay to help raise them. Even after all they'd been through, Ellie was still yearning to know more about him, just like her brother, but the feeling seemed foolish at best. "Oh."

"Oh? 'Oh,' is all you're going to say?"

"What do you want me to say?"

"I don't know, but I think you'll be interested in what I found."

"Fine. What did you find?" She sat up in the bed, hunching over her diary as her fingers played along the small butterfly design etched into the cover.

"A picture of him having coffee with another man, almost twenty years ago."

"And this matters why?? I've had enough mystery in my life to last for the rest of eternity. Quit being cryptic and help me get the big picture here." She growled into the phone to give voice to her angst.

"Okay … put your teeth back in your head." He paused and mumbled something to the cat, she assumed. "The other man was your boss."

Ellie tried to let the information sink in, but really didn't have much capacity for the unexplored in her tiredness. "What do you mean, the other man was my boss?"

"Shit, Sis. Get some coffee, some sleep, some 5-Hour Energy. Stay with me. The other man in the picture, having coffee with Dad, twenty years ago, is your boss."

"How can you tell that?"

"First off, the picture of him looks just like Mr. Kelley. Secondly, I asked Mom."

Ellie slipped out of the bed, needing to pace the floor around the room. "You asked Mom? She told you that the man with Dad in the picture was David Kelley?"

"Yes, Ellie. She said that they were the best of friends and had been for years."

"Mom spoke today like she recognized the picture?"

"Yes, and she knew exactly who was in the picture, Elle. It was your boss."

"Twenty years ago? That would make him like fifteen or something. Was the other guy a kid?" She hated the breathlessness in her voice, but her mind was racing ahead of her with the realization that David was more than just a Balance Keeper; he was unchanging—immortal.

"No. The guy sitting across from Dad is a thirty-something-year-old man."

"Are you sure it's not David's father? Remember you were saying that his father looks just like him."

"That wasn't his father, Elle. That was him. Something is off with this dude. He's not aging, and he was friends with Dad. What have you found out so far?" Jacob was pacing now too, from what she could tell. The airy quality of his words gave her a sense of comfort that they were so much alike in so many ways.

"I've found out a lot, but there's a lot more to know. I'll tell you all about it when I get home, I promise." She sat down on the bed, exhausted by the thought of her dad knowing David. What did that mean? Was that part of why she was chosen?

"Just be careful. I love you and Mom does too. Text me tomorrow and let me know you're okay. There's something off about this character, and I don't want to sound crazy, but I think it has something to do with Dad. He might be a vampire, so no snuggling with him, you hear me?"

"Jacob, be for real," Ellie barked into the phone, almost berating him until she remembered that David was most certainly something besides human. "You're right … I'll be careful and will text you more tomorrow. Keep looking for information, and I'll spill everything when I get home on Tuesday."

"Only four more days. Be careful, Sis."

"I will," she whispered into the phone and turned it off. "What the hell does this all mean? It has to connect, but how?"

She texted Jacob, asking him to send her a picture of David and their dad together, seeing as how she'd never seen her father. If she were going to start putting together the pieces of the mystery, she might as well see what her old man looked like. She picked up her journal and thumbed through it to look for the entry she'd read the night before while she waited for Jacob's text.

The scene she'd recounted had been two men sitting together at a coffee shop, one of them talking as golden dust shimmered in between them. If David was the only one fighting for the light, did that mean the person she described was him? She couldn't make out his face in her memory, but she could see the other man clearly. He looked like Jacob, but surely she was simply assigning him those features after having spoken with her brother tonight. She was trying to make the entry in her journal match the picture Jacob spoke about, but without actually seeing the picture, she couldn't know for sure.

The phone dinged, and she picked it up, scrolling through the messages to the picture. A soft gasp left her lips as she made the image bigger. David was sitting across from the man she'd assumed to be a stranger, but was really her father. She moved her focus back to David.

"That's the man I've been working for, the one I kissed, the one I can't stop thinking about." She felt her heart shudder at her brother's next message.

1997, taken by Ellie, 7 years old.

She texted back, *I thought Dad left before we were born.*

Mom said he did and that you didn't know who you were taking a picture of … or did you?

Chapter **Fifteen**

The night was rough, and her dreams were tainted with terror. Ellie woke in a panic, the world that once sat just beyond her reach now seemed almost suffocating. If she could come up with a reasonable explanation for everything, she might manage to keep herself from breaking down in front of the first person who showed her kindness that morning. She had to talk to Jacob more. She needed to tell him everything, but doing it over the phone wasn't going to fly. She needed to see his reaction and judge her own sanity by it, much like she'd been doing since they were kids.

Every good idea, every bad one ... hell, every idea was run past her brother to see if he thought she should move forward or not. The fact that she rarely listened to him or heeded his advice wasn't the point, the point was to make sure that she considered things from all sides, and without him to talk to, she felt that her recent experiences were very one-sided. Leaning over the edge of the bed with her head in her hands, she calmly breathed in and out. David was definitely not human. That had been proven the day before when he used magic, or 'light' as Sandra had labeled it, to render several people unconscious and convince another to turn himself in for attempted murder.

Sandra wasn't human either, from what Ellie could tell. Or if she was, then she was a witch. How else could she see the future and know Jacob's name without being told? "A witch," Ellie murmured and stood up from the bed, her pajamas wet with the remnants of her night.

A long hot shower helped a little, and she worked hard at not thinking through everything that plagued her senses. David would be playing golf for most of the day, if she remembered correctly, and she wanted to do some shopping. People didn't come to LA and not take a day or so to go shopping. With the holidays right around the corner, now would be a perfect time for retail therapy and getting her family a few gifts. *Kill two birds with one stone.*

A note on her phone confirmed that David was with Victor. They were an odd combination. Ellie shrugged her narrow shoulders and tugged on a pair of black slacks, pulling a cream-colored sweater over her head and finishing off the outfit with a few perfectly placed flares of red. She adjusted her belt, slipped on her shoes and grabbed her bag on the way out. She knew it would be smart to check her bank account instead of running down to the main shopping district in LA without knowing what she could afford, but for today … she didn't care.

If she accepted the partnership David was offering her, then money would become someone else's worry. It had been hers for so long, ever since she'd been trying to pay off her school loans and take care of her mother's medical bills. Part of the reason she hated her father so much was the burden he'd placed on both her and her brother by not helping to financially support her mom. *Be nice to know why …*

She slipped into the elevator behind a young woman about her age, a smile touching her mouth as she nodded to the other girl. Funny how people stopped staying good morning after a certain age and just nodded their heads, like the person you were nodding to was supposed to read the gesture correctly. Ellie chuckled to herself and the girl looked over at her.

"Sorry, just thinking of something comical." Ellie smiled, trying to lighten the mood.

"No worries. I love your belt. Where did you pick it up from?" The girl bent over a little, her pixie blond hair bobbing at her movements. She reached out to touch Ellie's belt and then hesitated until Ellie nodded. *There's that dumb nod again.*

"I'm actually from New York, so I picked it up at the Macy's close to Times Square." Ellie moved back a little after the girl finished inspecting the belt.

"New York? How fun. I've not been there, but when I get through with my schooling here, I'm definitely going to check it out. Anyway, your outfit is awesome."

"Thanks." Ellie blushed and fidgeted with her sweater. "It's just something comfortable I threw together."

"Have fun today," the girl said over her shoulder as she exited the elevator, Ellie moving slowly behind her. She was getting lost in her thoughts again. The smell of the nearby bistro wrapped around her senses, and she stopped for a moment to consider a slight detour for something warm and yummy for breakfast.

"Hi, Miss Ellie. Are you heading out soon?" The driver they'd been using all week stood just inside the glass door, his black top hat and overcoat making him look as if he worked for the rich and famous. She almost felt silly standing there like a young girl with no clue of what to do next.

She coughed to cover up her thoughts and smiled. "Yes. I wanted to go to the shopping district today, but was caught up in thinking about breakfast, thanks to the great smells."

"Well, there's a fantastic bakery right by the large, outdoor mall downtown. How about I drop you off there, and then you can just round the block and shop until your heart's content?" He smiled and opened the door as she moved toward him.

"That sounds fantastic." She smiled and walked into the cool mid-morning air. Having forgotten to grab her jacket, she simply wrapped her arms around herself and moved quickly to the car. "Did David already leave to play golf?"

The driver waited until they were both in the car to answer. "Oh, yes. He and Mr. Romales shared the car this morning around seven a.m."

"Victor is staying here at the hotel?" Ellie asked, the surprise in her voice even giving her pause.

"Yes, ma'am. He usually stays in the same location as David. They are quite inseparable."

She sat back and let the man's words seep in, confusion moving across her thoughts. David and Victor were inseparable? Did Victor live in New York? Something about the last sentiment gave her a full body shiver. *Am I scared of him? He's beautifully dangerous … just like David.*

The driver's voice pulled her from her thoughts, and she focused on the various landmarks he spoke of. He was much more talkative without David in the car, and she actually enjoyed taking the scenic route and understanding better some of the history and past events that had occurred in LA.

"You know why Los Angeles is named the City of Angels, Miss Miller?" The driver asked as Ellie returned her attention to the back of his head.

"No, tell me."

"In 1781, a group of Spanish settlers founded the town and called it what, in English, means *The Town of Our Lady the Queen of Angels*." He smiled in the rearview mirror and she smiled back, the comfort of the moment giving her a break from the craziness that had become her life.

The car pulled to a stop along a busy street and the driver turned in his seat. "See that bakery right there on the corner, Tollep's?"

She turned to locate it and mumbled yes.

"Great. You have to try the pecan kolache. You'll love it, I'm sure. Haven't met a woman that didn't fall madly in love. Just call me when you're ready to be picked up and give me a location, and I'll be there. Good?" He smiled and moved to get out of the car, her door opening shortly thereafter.

She slipped out of the car and nodded. "Good. And I'll have to let you know if the kolache was all you promised it would be."

"Oh, it will be, no worries there."

She moved as he shut the door, and then she walked toward the large crowd of people that were making their way across the busy street. People of all ages, sizes and shapes molded together in a large amoeba to clear the street for oncoming cars as the sign changed from a walk signal to a halt. Ellie hustled herself the rest of the way through the crowd and onto the right side of the street.

The line outside of Tollep's was incredible, wrapping around the building once and threatening to do it again. She shrugged and got in line, quite surprised by how quickly it moved. People in LA must be in as much of a hurry as the people back in New York. She smiled at the thought and turned to listen to a young girl playing her violin on the corner of the street. Ellie reached into her purse and pulled out a couple of bills, bending over to drop them into the girl's case.

"Thank you." The girl didn't miss a beat, but picked up the pace and moved into a beautiful Christmas song. Ellie couldn't exactly put her finger on which song it was, but it was lovely and filled the air with something almost magical. A warmth spread across Ellie's midsection and chest, and she wrapped her arms around herself, almost worried that she might explode gold power everywhere. She reached up and brushed her finger quickly against her tongue, not wanting to bring any attention to herself, but needing to know.

Sure enough, the tip of her finger was coated in a golden dust, much like the stuff David put on display every time she watched him in action. Was the light something that accumulated inside people when they gave goodness to the world, or was it just her? She'd never heard of or seen anyone with this particular gift, or curse, as it were. Maybe it was just her and David that had it. How odd that fate had put them together. *Not fate, God.*

She rolled her eyes as she realized how silly she sounded. Her mother believed in God, and Jacob did too, but Ellie hadn't gotten over all the pain and sorrow of watching their mother waste away. Where was God in all of that? The warmth in her chest began to dissipate as the cold realization that her mom most likely wouldn't make it past the next year set in. How did someone lose both parents before they turned thirty and still find peace with an all loving and powerful creator? She had yet to accept that, but she knew her mother and Jacob would be ever persistent.

Thoughts of sadness and anger were swept aside as the liveliness of the small bakery was presented to her. She moved just inside the door, holding it open as a large, older man stepped up behind her and took a turn holding it. Teenage kids gathered in one corner of the bakery, most of them sporting chocolate milk mustaches and loving it. She laughed softly under her breath, wanting to be that age again, just to be silly for a few minutes. The workers behind the counters were moving as quickly as possible, and yet no one seemed to be in a foul mood.

Soft classic Christmas music played from the ceiling, and the shop was decorated in red and green, the tree being illuminated by plastic donuts that lit up. She took everything in as the smell of butter and floury goodness danced along her senses. Something about the holidays made her want to grab a few pastries and a cup of coffee and snuggle up. *How about a sexy man? After the coffee and pastries …*

She made her way to the front, noticing that the clerk was a guy in his late twenties just a bit older than her. His smile was wide, and the warmth in his eyes offered her peace she didn't expect to find or need.

"Morning. How can I help you today? Wanna try our new toffee nut latte with one of our world famous pecan kolaches?" He placed his hands on the counter and tilted his head a little as Ellie studied the board above her.

She looked down at him and smiled. "Actually, that's exactly what I want."

"Awesome. First one today to take my suggestion. I was beginning to think I was losing my touch here." He chuckled and rang her up. "Six twenty-five."

She pulled her money from her purse and laughed as well. "Well, if you did lose it, I'm thinking you just got your groove back." She moved to the other side of the counter where the pick-up section was and turned to continue to study the room full of people from different stations in life who were all drawing around the warmth offered by the atmosphere and the delicious baked goods.

"Some things in life are just universal, I suppose." The sound of a woman's voice beside her caused her to stiffen a little. Ellie turned and smiled, recognizing the lady from David's party, but not remembering her name.

"Beg your pardon?" Ellie said politely.

"You had that look on your face. You know, the one that says you see peace in this place and that it's pretty unique for people to share something so rare." She shrugged and turned to put a cube of sugar in the dark liquid that moved about in the cup she held.

"That's exactly what I was thinking." Ellie crossed her arms over her chest and turned to face the woman a little more. "Have we met? You seem very familiar to me."

"Yes. At David Kelley's party. I'm an old friend of his." She extended her hand and Ellie took it. "Veronica Mills."

"Oh yes, you're a talent agent here." Ellie finally got her bearings, some part of her wishing that she hadn't. The woman in front of her obviously had feelings for David, ones that he didn't seem to reciprocate.

"Yes, well, we all have to make a living somehow, I suppose." Her smile was genuine and more kind than Ellie remembered from the gala.

"I'd love to make my living helping the stars reach their place in the sky." Ellie chuckled and grabbed her kolache and coffee before starting to make the black liquid more golden, as it should be.

"Nice catchphrase. I might have to steal that off of you," Veronica said, laughing. She took a quick sip of her coffee. "I have to run, but I was hoping we could have dinner tonight. David rarely gets out here anymore, and from talking with Sandra, it seems as though you've been exposed to our world. Seems like we should get to know one another better while you're here."

Ellie sat her coffee down and tried to hide her shock. *Is everyone here in on this balance keeping stuff?* She nodded and took a bite of her kolache, truly unsure of what to say. The buttery sweetness rushed in to help take her mind off the uncertainty that lay before her. Who was normal? Who wasn't? What did normal even mean anymore?

"I take that as a yes? Dinner tonight?"

Ellie swallowed and nodded. "Yes, dinner tonight sounds great. I'll text David to make sure he's available."

"He is. I talked to him and Victor earlier this morning. How else would I know you'd be here?" She smiled and turned to walk out, Ellie taking another bite of her pastry as she watched her go. The woman was way too beautiful to compete with, but hopefully David was speaking the truth when he admitted that Veronica wasn't his type.

"How else would she know I was here? How the hell did *he* know I was here?" Ellie sighed loudly and moved to a small, two person table by the window. She slipped into the tiny seat and enjoyed her breakfast far more than she thought possible. Dinner with David and Veronica tonight … *Great.*

Chapter **Sixteen**

Ellie made it back to the hotel with only an hour before their dinner date. She rushed upstairs with a few too many bags in hand and had trouble squeezing into the small opening the elevator provided. Luckily no one was there to witness her gluttony. She leaned against the back wall of the elevator and exhaled, letting the bags fall to the floor around her. The ride to the top wasn't long, but long enough that she could take a breather and let go of everything. David had called a few hours prior to give her an update on the dinner date. He didn't seem too surprised when Ellie informed him that Veronica had located her at the bakery that morning and invited her.

She wanted to ask him questions about Veronica's part in what seemed to be shaping up as the oddest crime fighting team she'd ever seen, but decided her timing was off. They'd agreed to meet at six sharp in the hotel lobby and ride together to the steakhouse his colleagues had chosen. He said it was a welcoming dinner for Ellie. She started to bring up that she hadn't accepted the partnership yet, but knew in reality that it was a moot point. She was falling for David, and something was changing inside of her that only he could help with. How much more cliché could you get?

The elevator door opened and the robotic voice announced, "Floor Eleven."

"Thank you," Ellie muttered toward the disembodied voice as she picked up her bags as best she could and shimmied through the opening. The walk to the room was quite clumsy, and yet she managed to get inside the door before tripping over a bag handle and doing a face plant. She rolled onto her back, lifting her feet in the air, and just laughed. It was one of those deep belly laughs that give rise to worry. Things were as odd as they'd ever been, and yet she was at peace because she understood more about David, which meant knowing more about her own past and future self.

"He knew my dad." Her voice fell flat, the laughter dying with it. "I wonder if he knows that."

Her phone buzzed in her purse, just beside her head on the floor, and she rolled over, crumpling packages in the wake of her movements. It was a text from Krista.

> *Your brother must be following me. I've seen him 10 times this last week.*
> *I've been gone two days. It hasn't been a week.*
> *Is he following me?*
> *Yes. He's going to be the father of your children, duh.*
> *I'm disturbed that some part of me thinks that's hot.*
> *Me too. What are you up to?*
> *Heading home after work. I have to study more tonight for the bar exam. I take it in two weeks.*
> *Best of luck. I'm trying to survive the rich and famous.*
> *You probably fit in beautifully.*
> *Yes. I remind them of where they came from.*
> *Dumb. Be safe and tell your brother he can't have this until he puts a ring on it.*
> *Oh Lord … you tell him. You're the one seeing him everywhere.*
> *This is true. Love you.*

Ellie closed her phone and lay on the floor a few more minutes, her body sore and tired, but her chest filled with warmth again. She and Krista had been friends for longer than she could remember. She'd been with her when her mother was diagnosed and sat through various visits and treatments with her when they were both just girls, by the world's view. Jacob had always had a soft spot for Krista, but Ellie thought it was because he thought of her like another sister.

"Guess not," Ellie grumbled as she unwrapped her legs from the shopping bags and crawled out of the clutter. "Five-thirty? Hell!"

She jumped up quickly, rushing around the room in an uncouth panic as she tried to think of what to wear and how to do her hair. She stopped in front of the mirror and tugged at her long brown locks, trying to tell if her hair was shiny enough to be considered greasy or if she could pull off one more event before having to wash it again. "It's good enough."

She moved to the bathroom and touched up her makeup, worked her hair into a tight bun and slipped out of her shopping clothes and into a dainty black dress. Red heels and a squirt of perfume, and she was out the door. She barely made it downstairs by six. David was standing near the front window with his back to her, the suit he wore fitting him like a glove. She felt her breath catch, but carefully let it out as she approached him.

He turned and smiled at her and the room shimmered a little. "You look beautiful tonight. The doorman said you just barely made it back from shopping. I was going to give you a call and tell you to take more time if you needed, but here you are."

"What can I say? I'm efficient, if anything." Ellie laughed and took a few steps to stand at a comfortable distance in front of him.

"Not sure efficient does enough to describe you, but I'll leave it at that." He turned to nod toward the driver before offering his arm to Ellie and looking down at her. "Ready to go meet the rest of my partners?"

She nodded and walked outside with him, snuggling into him a little as the wind pushed against her. "So, Sandra and Veronica are your partners, much like you're asking me to be?"

David helped her get into the car before walking to his side and sliding in beside her. "Victor, Veronica and Sandra are all Balance Keepers and, as such, are my partners in this life we've been given."

"I'm not sure what to think about all of this, to be honest. I understand it's real and it's happening, but the logical side of my mind shuts it down rather quickly."

"That will all change as you come into your place among us." He reached over and squeezed her hand, leaving his hand on top of hers afterward. "I'll help you work through the kinks. I'd tell you more, but I think it's better if you try to work through things as you see and experience them. However, tonight has nothing to do with business and everything to do with celebrating your arrival. It's been a rough couple of years with only four of us."

"And who says I've decided to join your odd gang of freedom fighters?" She laughed and enjoyed the smirk that played along his perfect lips.

"Sandra said you would, and if you didn't agree, I'd simply ask Veronica to move back in time and change your mind. Simple really." He laughed, but she sat with a sour look on her face.

"So there was really no choice in the matter, as you led me to believe?" she said, the tone of her voice betraying the intensity that her words might otherwise portray.

"There is never a choice when you've been given a gift to use. You use it." He removed his hand and rubbed his palms along his thighs as he looked over at her. She couldn't help but notice that his hair was a bit messier than usual. "None of us had a choice when we were chosen to keep things in a state of equilibrium. It's a driving force in your life, and the creator doesn't rest until you respond to it."

"The creator, as in God?" Ellie hated the touch of angst that laced her words. She didn't want to share her sadness and disappointment where God was concerned.

"Whatever you like to call him, Ellie." David paused as if thinking. "Your future doesn't hinge on whether or not you believe in him or even like him. It hinges on his belief in you."

What does that even mean? She tried not to sigh out loud and instead decided to busy herself by watching the city's Christmas lights dance against the darkness of the sky. The fact that she was beginning to feel differently about David was almost overwhelming by itself, but throw in a different life and a future that made no sense ... and was she going to become immortal?

She looked over at him and was glad to find him busy texting someone. She stared at him from the corner of her eye, the intense gaze on his face causing butterflies to rise in her chest. Was he immortal? Was he the man that sat next to her father all those years ago? How, out of all the people in the world, could she take a picture of her own dad and the man she'd one day start to fall for and not know it?

Her thoughts moved to the conversation she'd had the day before with Jean Pierre when he'd told her the story of how he was rescued by David when he was no more than a boy. It was doubtful that another boy could have saved Jean if he were drowning. No, David was a man then, and he was a man when he was with her father. He was that same man today.

"How old are you, David?" she couldn't help but ask, hating it the minute she let it leave her lips.

He looked up, tilting his head a little as he stared at her. "How old do I look, Elle?"

She tried to make light of it, but failed miserably. "You look no more than thirty-five, I suppose, but I'm thinking that's not exactly the right answer."

The side of his mouth lifted a little and he winked at her. "You would be right."

The rest of the ride was taken in silence, David texting back and forth with someone and Ellie sitting back, lost in the implications of all of this new information. A dinner to welcome her into a partnership with people that she didn't know, who did things that she was sure she couldn't and believed in a way of life that allowed the supernatural to reign. *What am I doing here?*

The driver turned and smiled at Ellie and David. "We're here, Mr. Kelley. What time should I pick you and Miss Miller up tonight?"

"A couple of hours should be fine." David moved out of the car, offering his hand to Ellie as she took it and moved in beside him. They walked to the restaurant together, the silence comfortable between them. The doorman held the door, and Ellie moved in behind David as he spoke to the hostess at the front of the room. The decorations were elaborate and screamed of royalty. Large, golden trees decorated the room, along with brilliant streams of ribbon and sparkling lights.

The sound of talking and laughter filled her senses, and she reached out to take David's offered hand as they walked through the dining hall. He looked back at her, a smile on his face, and she welcomed the reassurance greedily. Perhaps it was the lighting in the room, or the broad span of his shoulders, or maybe the dark promise in his gaze, but something had her feeling rather lightheaded. By the time they made it to the table she needed her chair for stability.

"There you are." Sandra stood and moved to offer David a quick hug as Ellie slipped into her seat, her eyes moving to Victor, who sat across from her quietly. David spoke to Sandra and Veronica and then sat down next to Ellie, reaching over to squeeze her forearm as a sign of support. Victor had yet to remove his ocean-blue eyes from her, leaving her feeling very dissected.

"Victor, tell Ellie here how our golf game went this morning, hmm?" David smiled, pulling his napkin into his lap and placing his elbows on the table.

Victor only broke his stare long enough to smirk at David before returning the weight of his attention to Ellie. "David is quite the golfer, but he barely pulled off a win. Some of us are far too busy with changing the world to perfect a simpleton's game." He shrugged and Ellie turned to watch David's reaction.

"Sore loser." David smiled and waved down the waiter as Ellie turned to greet Veronica and Sandra.

"How was your shopping today?" Veronica asked, but she cut Ellie off before she even had the chance to respond. "Sandra, Ellie and I met this morning for pastries down at Tollep's, and then the little tart got to shop all day long."

Sandra smiled and reached across David to squeeze Ellie's hand. "How dare you and V go to Tollep's and not invite me. It takes effort to stay this buxom."

Ellie laughed in spite of herself, wanting to correct Veronica and say that they hadn't *met* anywhere, but figuring it might not be the best start to what was probably going to be a long dinner. "The pecan kolaches down there are delicious. The driver today told me they would be, but they were beyond anything I could ever imagine."

David motioned for the group to order drinks, and then he ordered them a few appetizers while Sandra and Veronica began to chat. Ellie found herself unable to not look across the table at Victor, who had remained relatively quiet. He turned from looking out across the restaurant and focused on Ellie, a smile touching his thin lips. He was like a dark prince standing out among rather commonplace people. David was breathtaking, but in a very varsity football player type way. Victor reminded Ellie of the perfect specimen of a beautifully seductive Dracula.

"You look stunning tonight, as if you didn't know." He spoke so softly that she almost assumed he hadn't spoken at all. The dark line that had pulsed around him a few days before was nowhere to be found, and yet the air shimmered, like a small gray cloud of dust before him. She wanted to reach over to test its existence, but didn't want to draw attention to herself. Besides, she was growing rather tired of looking like a small child trying to find her way around a new place.

"Thank you," she murmured and looked toward David.

He leaned in toward her. "Thank you for what?" He smiled and she shook her head, trying to think of something that might make sense. Had he not heard Victor? The man's voice was subtle, but she'd heard him quite clearly.

"Thank you for bringing me here tonight. It should be a lot of fun." She smiled and moved back in her seat, her eyes flittering toward the one dark spot at the table and wondering why he intrigued her so.

"Of course." David turned to look at everyone else. "I know we're not going to talk about business tonight, but while we're all here I want to explain to Ellie and to all of you what my plans are to get her up to speed on who we are and what we do."

"Is that not all inherently ingrained in who she is? Knowing who we are and what we do as well as how she fits into all of it?" Veronica spoke up, the slight iciness from the night before slipping into her words.

"No. She's different than us because she's second generation. Without going too much into detail, let me explain further." David paused as their drinks arrived and a few plates of various tapas were laid on the table.

"Second generation, yes … I'd almost forgotten about her connection to Jacob." Victor winked at Ellie as she looked up, a little shocked to hear her brother's name on his lips.

Chapter **Seventeen**

"The plan will be for Ellie to spend the next month with me, working on gaining strength and understanding of my gift. We'll compare our abilities at the end of the month, and if she is the Core, as I suspect she is, then she will spend next month with you, Sandra, back here in LA." David paused as Ellie spoke up.

"Wait ... why would you assume that I am the Core, and what does that mean again?"

Victor leaned forward, his eyes full of knowledge and apparent age. "It means that you share in all of the gifts given to each of us. There always has to be one Balance Keeper that has all the gifts. It's a failsafe of sorts."

"It also means that if something happens to one of us, you can fill in as a quick back-up, seeing that you can do what each of us can do," Veronica added before picking up her glass and taking a long drink.

"And you guys really believe that I could be the Core? Why? Seems ridiculous to me." Ellie scoffed, her shoulders raising in a defensive manner.

David reached over and touched her knee, a kind look in his eyes. "I simply think it's possible. We won't know anything until the end of the month. It's obvious that you share my gift of whispering for the light. The question is whether you share in the other gifts found around the table."

Ellie touched her lips absently, her focus on the table before her as she thought through the implication of his words. "The gold dust?"

"Yes. It's the goodness inside of me that the creator put there to transform a situation from bad to good. I can whisper, or breathe life, from my very essence. I saw it on your lips as well today." David moved his hand and motioned for everyone to start enjoying the appetizers.

Ellie didn't move toward the food, but looked over toward David, her hands finding a place to lie in her lap. "I saw it in the air in my bathroom too. I was beginning to wonder if I accidently inhaled some of it when we were helping Gen this morning."

"No, that was created by the gift that's been placed inside of you. Over the next year you'll recognize more and more where your gifts lie."

David turned his attention toward the food for a few moments and Sandra spoke up. "We know for sure that you're either the Light Whisperer, as David has been for a very long time, or you're the Core. No two people can share the same gifts except the Core and each of us. So the question, over the next short while, will be which of you is the new Core." She pointed between David and Ellie, everyone nodding in agreement.

The weight of the conversation took its toll on Ellie's appetite. She excused herself a few minutes later to go to the ladies' room to freshen up. The pressure of being something more than what she was yesterday was a bit overwhelming. Once safe in the overtly fancy restroom, she sat down on the toilet seat and pressed her forehead to her fingers, trying to just get a grip on things.

"Why is this happening? Why me?"

It seemed to be the one question no one could answer, or perhaps they weren't willing to. It had to have something to do with her father. She needed to understand the picture of her dad and David together. *I'll ask him later tonight, after dinner. Surely if this has to do with my father he'll tell me.*

Or maybe her mother knew something. Ellie would have to tell Jacob everything, which was going to be hard and yet a huge relief. To share all of this with someone that loved her unconditionally and would help her dig deeper to figure it out, not to mention help her come up with a plan for the future, was exactly what she needed. "Yeah, like now."

She sat there for a few more minutes, the warm air of the heat blowing hard along the back of her exposed neck. Calm surrounded her, and the panic that seemed to be setting in too often lately was driven away. Everything would be fine. If she was intended to be a Balance Keeper or a Whisperer of the Light, then she would do it—and well. The gift she'd seen David use that morning was powerful and almost overwhelming, but it was warm and welcoming too. There was a sense of rightness to it, like nothing she'd ever experienced before.

She rejoined the group a few minutes later with a smile on her face and she redirected the conversation toward lighter topics. She'd spend the next month with David and then a month with Sandra and do whatever else she needed to do to figure things out. She was on a mission to uncover who David was and what that meant to her, as well as who she was now. Funny how she'd shifted from wanting to know him to now needing to know him. It seemed as though he might be the key to getting to know herself.

"Dinner was great." Ellie looked over toward David next to her in the car as they returned to the hotel. The rest of the meal had been fantastic, and the celebration that took place made her feel welcomed and more at ease. With a few glasses of wine in her, Veronica had melted a little more and was almost funny and endearing. Victor had loosened his tie a little and stopped staring so intently at Ellie, and the sound of his laugh made the room light up and her heart skip a beat. She had found her eyes landing on him more often than she wanted. Meanwhile, Sandra had kept the jokes flowing and reminded everyone of various stories from their past. Ellie knew nothing of these stories, but she'd enjoyed them all the same.

"Yes, it was. You were great." He reached over and squeezed her hand, his fingers lingering a little too long on her skin. He moved his hand back, coughing softly into it before looking out the window. "We have a lot of work to do, but I feel like this is going to be good for all of us."

"I'm all in." Ellie leaned back against her seat, a smile touching her lips at the admission of being willing to be or do whatever they needed. Life wasn't going to be the same, but it seemed as though this gift, or new life, wasn't something that one chose, but that it chose you. So, did she really even have a choice in the matter?

"I'm glad to hear that. We'll begin working again when we get back to New York next week." He paused for a few minutes and then turned toward her a little. The darkness of the car allowed the shadows to bathe across his features, making him appear even more imposing, if possible. He looked devilishly handsome and demanded her attention as he simply let his eyes move across her.

"What?" she mumbled, her chest tightening uncomfortably.

He reached out and let his fingers brush along the soft curve of her cheek, his eyes following his own movements like a predator waiting for the perfect opportunity to pounce. "I'm proud of you. That's what."

She smiled and reached up to capture his hand in hers, pressing her cheek against the warmth of his large fingers. "I don't think I have much of a choice in the matter. Do you?"

He smiled and moved his hand back. "No, you actually don't. Once you're chosen, that's it. It would drive you mad not to be a part of us."

"One question you still haven't answered is why me?"

He nodded, his features shifting slightly to appear almost non-committal. "I know. It's not a conversation we're having tonight either, but it is one we'll have soon. I promise."

She sighed softly, but let it go and worked to get her coat together as the car pulled to a stop. She slipped out behind him and took the offering of his hand.

"You look beautifully ridiculous."

She looked up and laughed. "I'll take that as a compliment."

"Come with me to my room for a nightcap. I want to talk a little more about what happened with you and Sandra. Are you up for it?" he asked, looking over his shoulder at her as they walked into the warmth of the hotel.

She felt her cheeks burn a little, the idea of being alone with him in his room causing more than images of a nightcap to appear. "Um, sure."

They moved into the elevator and he pressed the button for his floor before beginning to work on the buttons of his black jacket. He held the door for her, and they moved in silence to his room as he fumbled with the card reader a little. She almost laughed at how ridiculous the moment had gotten, but remembered that perhaps it wasn't the best time to be comical. Would something happen between them? Their kiss the first night still lingered in her mind, and his small touches and signs of affection had been there all week long. Did he feel the way she did?

"Come on in and feel free to make yourself comfortable." David moved in behind her, and she saw that his room was an exact replica of her own. He dropped his items on the bed and made his way toward the mini-bar, beginning to work on pouring them something to drink. Ellie slipped out of her shoes and laid her jacket on the bed next to his. She tugged at her hair and almost sighed with relief as it fell from its prison and swept along her back.

She opened the curtains and stared out the window for a minute, the city full of life for as far as her eyes could see. "I bet it's snowing in New York tonight. I love the cold weather at home, but it's nice to not be in the middle of a blizzard."

"I couldn't agree more," he mumbled, walking toward her with her drink extended in front of him.

She took it and moved back as he opened the balcony doors, a cool breeze meeting them as they walked out. She slipped into a small wooden chair and crossed her legs, the slow burn of the liquor adding to her sense of comfort. David sat down beside her; from the messy look of his hair, it was obvious he'd just dragged his fingers through it.

"What do you want to know about my time with Sandra?" Ellie's voice was soft and almost childlike.

He sat back and shook the ice around in his glass as he looked out into the distance and then back toward Ellie. "Tell me anything you want to. I'm just curious how you're holding up, to be honest. I've never known another life than this one, but I know you have."

Ellie reached down to set her glass on the ground beside her before tucking her legs up into the chair with her. "I'm fine with everything Sandra said. Everything is changing around me, and accepting that helps me to get through the next 'what the hell' moment. I'm not interested in talking about Sandra."

"Then what do you want to talk about, Ellie?" His voice softened just a little, causing a shiver to run through her.

"I want to talk about us. Or, really, you. I want to know why you listed my name as your password at the airport, for starters."

A smile touched his lips. "It's about time."

She laughed and let her feet drop to the ground, sitting up and rolling her shoulders. "I know. I just didn't want to sound crazy in front of you, but seeing as how you puff gold dust like a magic dragon …"

"Hey, now." He chuckled again. "I put your name as my password because I knew you'd be running late that night and thought it might help get you through the gate faster."

"When did you change your password to my name, David?"

"Four years before you came to work for me." He took a drink of his drink. "Sandra called the day I changed it and told me the future, or parts of it. I knew that you'd need proof that something odd was happening around you, something to draw you in deeper as you worked to figure me out."

"So you changed the password four years in advance of us meeting because you knew I'd be stunned by the timing?"

"Yes, and I made a bloody mess on my floor with a deer carcass because I needed you to want to know more about me." He paused and turned to face her a little more. "The morning you came in a few weeks ago and I was in my office covered in blood, frantically cleaning it up ..."

"That was a deer?" She covered her face with her hands and laughed sarcastically. "And here I thought you were a murderer."

"Not in the sense you might have thought."

She dropped her hands and looked over at him. "You pretended to murder someone so that I'd start stalking you? You realize how crazy that is, don't you?"

He laughed and the sound wrapped around her as golden dust shimmered in the air around them. "Yes. I wish I had a better answer for you, but I knew you'd want to know more once you saw that. I'm just glad you're finally owning up to stalking me."

She couldn't help but smile, a sense of relief washing over her at the verification that he wasn't a murderer. The pieces were falling together quickly now. All of the supernatural things that had led up to her believing in his gift had been planned to bring her into this new reality more quickly.

"You planned the flowers and the note." She looked back toward him.

"Yes. Sandra helped me plan every bit of it and ran into the future to see if it would all work. It took lots of work, but we knew we'd need you in place by the time your gifts developed, so we simply took tons of precautions." He shrugged, finished his drink and stood, leaning against the railing and focusing somewhere in the distance.

"Brilliant," she mumbled and stood to join him. "Did you just say that Sandra 'ran into the future'?"

He looked over at her. "Yes. She can move along the lines of time into the future, just as Veronica can move along the lines of the past."

"And Victor?" Ellie asked, curiosity getting the best of her.

"He is my polar opposite."

She thought for a few moments, trying to decide what it might mean to be David's polar opposite. "You mean he whispers as well?"

"Yes, but where I am the light ..." he let his words fall short and she finished them for him.

"He is the darkness."

"Yes," David said softly, standing and running his fingers through his dark hair. "I feel sorry for him, but he does the job that was given to him and has for a very long time."

The idea of getting to put good into the universe left one feeling warm and comfy, but having to spew evil and darkness? *How horrible.* She shivered, and David put an arm over her shoulder, pulling her in to his side. She had one more question that needed to be answered.

"I know you said now wasn't the time, but I need to know. Why me, David? Does it have something to do with my father?"

He moved a little, standing to his full height and pulling her toward him in a hug she hadn't expected. She slipped her arms around his neck and looked up at him, the moonlight tugging at parts of her she'd forgotten existed. He was ethereal and beautiful, almost otherworldly, and he was someone she could easily spend the rest of her life chasing after.

He brushed a stray strand of her hair behind her ears and pressed his forehead against hers before speaking in a voice too low for most to hear. "I did know him, and I'll tell you all about him when the time is right. Change is coming, and I think dealing with one thing at a time is best."

She didn't wait for him to move. Moving her hands to cup his cheeks she lifted to her tiptoes and pressed her lips to his, tilting her head a little to gain more access to his decadent mouth. He groaned and wrapped his arms around her tightly, his palm cupping the back of her head as they enjoyed an intimate moment together. He pulled back a little, kissing her softly one more time to seal the deal and shook his head.

"You're going to be the death of me, Ellie." He kissed her once more and moved back, and she felt the loss of his warmth immediately.

"Why is that?" She smiled, her lips still tingling from the pressure and aggression of his kiss.

He picked up his glass and moved into the room, holding the curtain open for her to follow. "I don't know the rules about what we can and cannot be right now, but there are some."

She felt an odd tightness in her chest. "What do you mean, rules as far as you and I are concerned?"

He closed the door behind her and moved toward the door to his room. "The universe being in balance is our calling in life. If I invest my emotions in something other than that, then I have a chance of getting the message wrong and shifting things for the worse. I've kept to myself for a long time, simply because of lessons learned when I was younger."

Ellie tried to swat away the sting of rejection that she shouldn't be feeling, but couldn't escape. She gathered her shoes, put her glass down and nodded at him as she walked toward the door. "Who was she?"

He looked down toward the ground and reached to open the door for her. "No one I care to talk about. Get some rest and tomorrow we'll meet with the Kepeners. You'll love them."

She stopped in front of him and reached up to touch his face, a sad smile on her lips. "Thanks for the celebration and a great night."

He simply winked at her before closing the door behind her. Against her will, her eyes filled with tears. What had she expected? That they'd get lost in each other's arms? *Would've been nice. What an odd ending to the night …*

She walked to the elevator and found relief in slipping in as the door opened to emptiness. Her joining up to help keep balance in the world was a tall order, but finding a way to do it without the promise of something becoming of her and David? *Impossible.*

Her thoughts bombarded her as she made her way back to her room, the heaviness of exhaustion sitting on her shoulders. She wanted to go home and just curl up with Marx and watch TV, to just get back to normalcy and leave this craziness behind. She laughed, but the sound fell flat as she walked into her room and let her shoes fall from her fingers.

"So, he isn't a murderer and he can't see into the future." She pulled off her clothes and fell into bed with the lights still on. "Those jobs belong to other members of the team."

Chapter **Eighteen**

The incessant screaming of her phone woke her the next morning; the hope that it would stop died as it rang for the twentieth time. She rolled across the bed and grabbed it, not caring to see who it might be before barking loudly into the small contraption.

"What?"

"Oh, thank God. Sis ... it's Mom."

As if cold water had been poured through her system, Ellie came to and cupped the phone, sitting down on the side of the bed and leaning into it. Her brother sounded horrible, the shaky timbre of his voice informing her quickly of what his words solidified.

"What's wrong? Jacob, is she okay?"

"No, Elle. She went into a coma this morning. She's forgotten how to eat and having trouble remembering to breathe."

"Remembering to breathe? I thought your body did that automatically." She felt like she might throw up, fear reaching up and snuffing out any early morning high a good night of rest might have provided.

"It does until that part of your brain gets affected by disease."

The sound of him sniffling caused her to lose her breath. She moved the phone from her ear and closed her eyes as tears welled up and a familiar burning set fire in her chest. She needed to get home. She couldn't lose her mother.

Not while she was in LA, chasing after a new life and a man who wasn't even available to her. She heard Jacob calling her and pulled the phone back to her ear.

"Can you just come home, please?"

"Yes. I'll be on the first flight out of here. Tell her to hold on, okay."

"Okay, Elle. I love you."

"I love you too." She dropped the phone on the bed and jumped up, rushing around the room to throw her stuff into the open suitcase that sat on the floor by the window. The knocking on the door behind her caused her to yelp, and she rushed over to open it. David stood there with a coffee in his hand and a knowing look on his face.

"Let me help you pack." He moved into the room, ignoring the fact that she was in her panties and a small undershirt. She grabbed her jeans and a t-shirt as he moved into the room, grabbing stuff and setting it in her bag. "She's going to come out of this."

"Oh yeah? How do you know that?" She stopped and put her hands on her hips, her tone almost mean. She needed someone to abuse, thanks to all the confusion in her life, and now another curveball was headed her way.

"Sandra called a few minutes ago to let me know that your mother was in a coma, but that she'd be out of it in two days. I'll help you pack and take you to the airport myself if you want. Don't worry about a thing. I'll be home on Wednesday, or I can come now if you want me to." He continued to pull things from the floor and tables around them.

She sighed and felt her emotions riding high. She already trusted Sandra's judgment. She suddenly felt so blessed, knowing that everything was going to be okay.

"Oh, thank God," she whispered and pressed her fingers to her eyes as tears started to drip down her face again. The warm wrap of David's arms gave her something to sink into as he held her and let her cry, softly whispering against her hair as he spoke reassuring things. She cried for a few more minutes before pulling back and wiping at her eyes.

"I'll go with you. We'll reschedule my meeting out here, or I'll get Veronica to bring me back to the past to fix those things that need my attention later." He moved back and reached for the coffee, offering it to her.

She took it and shook her head. "No. If my mom's going to be fine then you finish up here, and I'll go home to help Jacob with her. I'll see you on Wednesday when you get back."

They chatted a little more about plans for later that week and Ellie finished packing. David helped to get her down to the front of the hotel and gave her a long hug goodbye. It was almost painful to leave his side, and yet she was still overwhelmed with concern for her mother. Knowing she would come out of it was one thing, but imagining the trauma of what she might be experiencing was another. As she headed to the airport, Ellie silenced her thoughts, leaning back and humming to the melodramatic version of "Silent Night" that played on the radio.

The airlines were more than accommodating when Ellie reached the ticketing booth, David having already called ahead to work everything out. She got her ticket and rushed toward the gate, since the plane had already boarded and was ready to leave. After checking her bag at the gate she found her seat in first class and slipped in by the window, the older gentleman beside her already sound asleep. She checked her watch and realized that it was only almost six, far too early for most people to be up and flying anywhere.

The stewardess checked on her, promising to bring back coffee and a small menu of food items that Ellie could choose from. She texted her brother that she was on her way and reclined her seat, the sun beginning to rise just outside her window. With everything that she'd been through this last week, this was the thing that was plaguing her most. Her mother's situation was outside of her control, and it would be only a matter of time until she lost her. Tears stung her eyes again, and she pushed them away with her fingertips, not wanting to appear emotional in front of a plane full of strangers.

Worry clouded her thoughts as the plane lifted in the air and she felt the pressure applied by the plane. Was her mother's life in the hands of the Balance Keepers like Gen's had been or was that just when someone was in a traumatic situation? Wasn't this traumatic? What if the balance was in favor of the light? Would Sandra have to make the call and decide that her mother wouldn't be allowed to be saved by David, but killed by Victor? Is that the way it worked?

Her heart shuddered in her chest as she recalled Mr. Pierre's words when David informed him that there was too much darkness in the world.

Oh, thank God …

What if it wasn't Sandra, David or Victor that had to make that decision and snuff out a life? What if it was to be her? What if she was the Core?

Stark awareness spread through her chest at the very weight of such a calling. She closed her eyes and coughed softly, wetness covering her fisted hand. Ellie knew what she'd see there before she witnessed it, but she needed the validation, so she glanced down warily.

Covering the top of her fist was a shimmery black glitter, the gift of darkness to match the essence of light that lay deep inside of her.

Acknowledgements

To my God, who loves me unconditionally even though I don't come close to deserving it. He's my inspiration and my greatest joy in life.

A quick thank you out to my first readers: My wonderful mother and my good friend, Jeanette. They take my mess and give me feedback right after the first draft, ignoring the horrid spelling and commas galore.

My editor Nicole, who also takes a beautiful disaster (my writing) and turns it into something that's not only legible, but consistent, building in plot strength and colorful. She's a gem and I couldn't be more blessed.

To my best friend, Rachel – the cover model for the book. She keeps me laughing and gives me grace far too often. She's everything I could ask for in a best friend. It was far too fun having her beautiful face as the centerpiece for my story.

To my beta readers! I love your thoughts & comments. You make the process better and I appreciate your time and dedication to my work.

To my family who blesses me beyond belief. Not sure how I got so lucky, but because of you, I love being me.

Lastly… to my readers. Thank you for taking the time to pick this brain-child up. My muse was chomping at the bit to write Ellie and I'm glad we did. I hope you find a place of reprieve to run away to within the context of my writing. I love to read for that very reason. Thank you for your support!

About the Author

Kate Thomas is the author of the Equilibrium Series, a five-book supernatural new adult series, with plans for a few more series in 2015.

She is a CPA by trade, a church planter and entrepreneur at heart; however, writing and reading are passions she just can't help but indulge in. With more ideas than one person should be allowed, she is blessed to have a muse that doesn't seem to take a vacation and more energy that one might consider healthy.

She writes under the following pen names:
L.A. Starkey - Young Adult & Middle Grade Paranormal
Isabella James - Sci-fi/Fantasy

For more information about the upcoming releases by Kate please join her mailing list:
http://eepurl.com/9Nrc1

The Light, Equilibrium II is scheduled to release May 2015!!

Enjoy the Book? Want More?

Check out these other great titles by Kate under her pennames:

The Soul Keeper Series by L.A. Starkey. Deceived (Book I), Destroyed (Book II) and Descent (Book III). This YA Paranormal series is a modern day love story about the implications of having more than one soul mate, and having to choose between the two of them. The decisions of the gods has left the next generation, their heirs, torn between fate and reality, and the balance of the future hangs in anticipation of what's to come.

 Resounding Truth by Kate Thomas. Derik has been the Alpha of the Graybacks since the death of Drucilia's father, his murder still weighing heavy upon Dru. With fierce determination and an iron fist, the new Alpha has successfully kept them alive and fed, but the threat of Hunters and Vampires creeps ever so close. With his eye on Dru as a prime candidate for his mate, he demands more than she's willing to give and blazes a trail of rage across the pack at her denial.

They have waited for a savior, for someone to come and take power from Derik and the time draws near. Dru's sister Karis can see deep into the future and makes it known that a white wolf will be their redeemer, but will he be too late? With the Queen of the vampires thirsty for an accord in blood and the head Huntress of the Circle of Elders seeking the white wolf with fever, things get tense and complicated far before the resounding truth is uncovered. Resounding Truth.

www.ingramcontent.com/pod-product-compliance
Lightning Source LLC
Chambersburg PA
CBHW020952180626
46814CB00003B/1060